SERVING SUGGESTIONS

SERVING SUGGESTIONS

Stories by

Michael Carson

LONDON
VICTOR GOLLANCZ LTD
1993

First published in Great Britain 1993
by Victor Gollancz Ltd

A catalogue record for this book is available
from the British Library

ISBN 0 575 05436 0

The following stories were first broadcast on BBC Radio 4: 'The
Punishment of Luxury'; 'Blow-Pipe'; 'The Sentence'; 'A Day by
the Sea with Mr Shukry'; 'On Fire for Guy'; 'The Consolation
Bridges Bring'; 'Supply Sides'; 'Even the Mice Know'; 'Percy
Wordsworth's First Chapter'; 'Travel is the Greatest Freedom';
'Yaohan's Sarong'; 'Ms Clip Inspects Ofingi'; 'Guest Workers';
'The Buddha's Mattress'; 'The German Cuckoo'; 'Untaken by
Angels'; 'This Sentence Does Not Consist of Eight Words'; 'The
Age of Reason'; 'The Automatic Door-Closer'; 'The Devil and
Mrs Fox'; 'Pitcher Plants'.
'Worried About Dolores' first appeared in *The Ten Command-
ments*; 'Serving Suggestion' first appeared in *Critical Quarterly*;
'Peter's Buddies' first appeared in *Gay Times*; 'On the Left Side'
first appeared in *Soho Square 4*.

Typeset at The Spartan Press Ltd
Lymington, Hants
and printed in Great Britain by
St Edmundsbury Press Ltd, Bury St Edmunds, Suffolk

For
Barbara Crowther
Sheila Fox
Duncan Minshull

Contents

Untaken by Angels

'The idea is,' said Benson to Eric as Eric fed slivers of celery through the wire to his huge rabbit. 'The idea is,' Benson repeated, frowning as Eric said how much Fluffy loved celery. 'The idea is that you write down a list in your very best handwriting and then send it up the chimney.'

'What happens after that?' asked Eric who, now that the celery had gone, was pushing his finger through the wire. 'I'm sorry, Fluffy, but I've run out. Oww!'

Fluffy had nipped Eric's finger.

'Serves you right for not listening to me,' asserted Benson unsympathetically. 'Anyway, you pay too much attention to that fat rabbit, if you want my opinion. My dad says that there are people starving all over the place and all you can do is feed that overfed creature perfectly good food.'

'What happens when the letter gets to the top of the chimney?' Eric asked, frowning at his finger. 'Maybe I should hold it under the tap.'

'Well, when the letter gets to the top of the chimney, an angel collects it and delivers it to the North Pole in the blinking of an eye.'

'Then what?'

'The angel gives it to Father Christmas and he goes around his ice palace collecting the order. Then he delivers it on Christmas Eve.'

Eric nodded.

'There is a hitch though,' added Benson, for whom everything in life had a hitch.

'What's the hitch?'

'You've got to be a good boy. That may be a bit difficult in your case.'

'I *am* a good boy!'

Benson gave Eric the quizzical look he had learnt from Sister Paul of the Cross at the convent school he attended.

'If you are such a good boy, how come I saw you riding your fairy cycle on the pavement the other day; if you're such a good boy, how come you had to pay a fine when you took your books back to the library last week; if you're such a good boy, how come God let you be born a Methodist instead of a Catholic? Sister Paul of the Cross says that anyone who says he is a good boy had better watch out. The Avenging Angel is oiling his wings to swoop down and test your metal!'

Eric stared back at Benson blankly, the nearest he ever got to a real protest. He decided to change the subject.

'Do you think I should write my address on the letter to Father Christmas?' Eric asked.

'Well, it can't do any harm. But Father Christmas is Saint Nicholas and saints don't need addresses.'

Both boys adjourned to their respective dining room tables to compose a winning letter to Father Christmas.

Benson could hardly wait for Mum to light the fire in the evening. As the December light faded, he shivered pointedly once or twice and, this having no effect, he sidled up on the subject by mentioning how cold it was for the time of year. This too failed and Benson decided to take a direct approach.

'Mum . . .' he whined.

'Don't you say another word!' snapped Mum as she poured batter over sausages and cabbage which would, by some strange alchemy, shortly be turned into her prize-winning Toad in the Hole.

'I only said "Mum" Mum,' murmured Benson.

'And no cheek either, young man!' snapped back Mum. 'I

know exactly what you want. You want the fire on so that you can send letters to·Father Christmas up the chimney.'

'How did you know?'

'Eric's mum says that Eric has been slaving away over his Christmas letter all afternoon. You know he's a bit slow with his writing, poor little mite.'

That was typical of Eric, Benson thought. He just could not keep anything under his hat. In that Eric was very different from Benson. Benson kept a great deal under his hat – a great deal more than fitted comfortably. Sometimes his secrets gave him a headache.

Benson, seeing that there was nothing to be gained by pleading, beat a hasty retreat and passed the time by re-reading his shopping list to Father Christmas. He went over the blue writing with a green crayon to make sure it would stand out and catch Father Christmas' eye straight off. Had he asked for too much? he wondered. No, he did not think so. He deserved a good stack of presents after all the sacrifices he had made that year, didn't he? What other boy of nine had given up sweets for the whole of Lent? Who else had accepted the slings and arrows of outrageous teachers without complaint? Had one other human being in the whole history of the world posted his pocket money – every penny of it – *on at least four occasions in the past year* into the Black Baby box chained to the life-sized crucifix at the back of English Martyrs' church? Benson felt strongly that the approach of Christmas heralded the pay-off for all his good deeds during the year. He did not doubt for a moment that a gaggle of messenger angels – angels whom he pictured looking like the man on National Benzol petrol pumps, only the angels wore frocks – would fly straight off to Father Christmas.

He perused his two-tone Christmas list again. A fairy cycle: well, that was hardly a luxury. With a fairy cycle he would be able to run messages for Mum more efficiently. He would also save her a fortune in bandages and Dettol resulting from wounds to his knee caused by his banging against the handlebars of his absurdly little tricycle. The Davey Crockett hat? That was necessary too. He could not gain admittance to Sean O'Shea's gang without a Davey Crockett hat. Yes, that was as necessary as a cap for a cub. The Meccano set – the one you could build Blackpool Tower out of – he had to have that. It would help him learn all kinds of skills, and with those skills he would be able to get a wonderful job and keep Mum in a manner to which she was unaccustomed. He would take her to see the Pope in Rome; have her groceries delivered from the posh grocer's shop that Mrs Ellis went to. A double Li-Lo Benson managed to justify because it was so much less selfish than a single one. With a double Li-Lo airbed he would be able to offer rides to less fortunate friends at the baths.

No, there was nothing on the list that could be interpreted as a luxury. Benson chewed on his crayon. Then, on the spur of the moment, he added: *A surprise*.

Later in the evening, when Mum had found time to light the fire, Benson went next door to Eric's. He knocked at the door and Eric's mum answered.

'Is Eric in, please, Mrs Jenkins?' asked Benson.

'I'll get him for you.'

'Thank you very much, Mrs Jenkins.'

Eric appeared carrying his letter and looking up at the smoke billowing out of Benson's chimney. The Jenkins family only had an electric fire with coals that looked as though they were burning but weren't. Benson had often pestered Mum and Dad to get one like that but, so far, they had resisted.

'Come on then!' commanded Benson.

The two boys approached the fire in Benson's lounge with their letters.

'What have you written?' Benson asked.

'Mind your own business!' Eric replied, mounting a rare rebellion.

'I didn't want to know anyway, Eric. Who cares what you've asked for? A doll's house, I shouldn't wonder.'

'I have not,' said Eric.

'Let's see then.'

'No!' And Eric started to fold his piece of paper.

'You can't do that! It'll never get up the chimney if you fold it.'

'Yes, but you'll look.'

'No, I won't! I promise,' lied Benson, crossing his fingers.

'Uncross your fingers and say that.'

Benson did so, but still Eric did not believe him. 'I want you to go outside while I put my paper up the chimney,' said Eric.

'Oh, all right. I'll push mine up first and then I'll go outside. I don't mind you seeing what I've asked for, though. Look.'

Eric looked but did not seem overly impressed. There was something odd about Eric today. He was just not his usual, slight, easily-manipulated self at all.

Without more ado, Benson lay his piece of paper over the fire and gave it a deft flick. The draught took the paper drifting out of sight and up the chimney. He could hear it scrape against the sides of the flue. Some soot dropped back into the grate.

'There. It's gone. Half way to the North Pole by now I shouldn't wonder,' said Benson proudly. 'It's certainly got a headstart on yours, Eric. If I were you I would get yours launched straight away, or you may be too late.'

'Go out then.'

Benson gave Eric his most severe *I am a Catholic while you are a mere Methodist* look and left the lounge without another word. In the hall he filled in the time of waiting by reaching up and opening the door of the cuckoo clock. The cuckoo came out and bent towards him, but did not make its ding-uckoo sound as it did when left to come out at the right time.

At last Eric emerged.

'Did you manage it?' Benson asked, hoping that Eric would have to abjectly request his assistance.

'Yes, thank you,' replied Eric, now more his usual pliant self.

Benson had not expected to be thanked for his services, and gave Eric a smile. He even managed to forgive him for his peculiar secrecy.

The next morning was a Saturday. A snow-drift pile of Christmas cards lay on the doormat of Benson's house. Benson picked them up and took them in to Mum.

'Good Lord!' said Mum when she saw the pile. 'I hope I've sent cards to everyone who's sent one to us.'

'Bet you haven't,' said Benson helpfully. He knew that Mum kept a store of spare cards to be sent off in a hurry to anybody who sent the Bensons one, but whom the Bensons had forgotten.

And, true to form, Benson was half an hour later pedalling up the road on the tricycle he had grown out of some years before. He carried six hastily written cards in the little basket on the front.

He returned puffed, wondering what to do next. Boredom sat on his shoulder and sighed into his ear. Benson crashed his tricycle into the garage door and mooned into the back garden where he dead-headed a few flowers with a garden cane. Then he saw a piece of paper lying on the grass. One of its edges was burnt. He approached it, a feeling of great trepidation aching into him. Could it be that the angel had failed to pick up his Christmas list? Could it be? No, he thought, it must be Eric's list. It had to be. After all, Eric was a Methodist. If one of the two papers had been rejected by the angel, it would have to be Eric's, wouldn't it?

Benson stood frozen in front of the paper, gazing down at it. He felt himself to be at the crossroads. The rejected request – was it his or Eric's? – would tell on whose side the angels stood. Once and for all he would know on whom God smiled. What if it were *his* letter?

After much jiggling about and many prayers, Benson knelt down to pick up the paper. His heart was beating in his head as he raised the paper and turned it over to reveal Eric's childish scrawl. He was about to feel great self-satisfaction, but then he found himself reading what Eric had written.

Dear Father Christmas,
MAKE MUM GET BETTER!
Thank you very much.
Eric

'Is Mrs Jenkins sick, Mum?'

'She's got a lump, son.'

'How do you mean?'

'It's hard to explain. You must just offer up some prayers for her. You've noticed how thin she is, have you?'

'Yes. It's cold today, isn't it, Mum? Could we light the fire?'

Surprisingly, Mum did not refuse, but obediently trailed the gas-poker from its source in the morning room, and soon the fire in the lounge was burning warmly.

Benson shut the lounge door, took Eric's paper out of his pocket, unfolded it and placed it over the fire. He prayed as hard as he could and flicked it up the chimney, calling on all the angels and saints to help him as he did so. The paper made its second journey up the chimney and Benson continued to pray as he went out to the front and looked up at the chimney. There was no sign of the note. He looked all around to see if it had floated back down to the ground, untaken by angels. He searched everywhere until he came to the part of the back garden on which the sun never shone. There, in the corner by the small shed where Benson never ventured because he had come to believe a wicked old man lived there who would carry him away, lay a white sheet of paper.

Benson did not hesitate. He felt angry and let down. How dare God not help Eric, he thought. How dare He not! He picked up the paper, turned it over and read:

A FAIRY CYCLE

A MECCANO SET

A DOUBLE LI-LO

A DAVEY CROCKETT HAT
A SURPRISE

He stared at the letter for several long moments. Then Benson looked up at the slate December sky, made silent pleas that surprised even him, pleas that turned to hard bargaining – and gave him a sudden pain – then tore up his letter to Father Christmas into very little pieces.

This Sentence Does Not Consist of Eight Words

'Can one get to the Tate Gallery North this way?' Harold asked the car park attendant.

'One can, if one wants to,' replied the man, looking past Harold to a ferry boat crossing the Mersey. 'But why would one want to? It's a load of rubbish. They only send us the dross. Bricks for the brickies.'

Harold thanked the car park attendant, though he would have preferred to throttle him. The cold wind blowing off the river seemed about to blow Harold's Auntie Annie away to join the kinetic Coke and special brew cans rolling drunkenly across the pier head. He linked her arm in a practical manner and wondered what he was doing there. My duty, that's what.

'That's typical Liverpool, isn't it, Annie?' Harold observed as he shepherded Auntie Annie through the wind tunnel between the harbour master's cottage and the Maritime Museum, en route to the Tate Gallery North.

Auntie Annie frowned. Just because Harold was in his forties and doing well down south, he should still ask before dropping Auntie from her name. 'How do you mean, Harold?' she asked him.

'Well, there he is meeting visitors all day. The Albert Dock is one of the biggest tourist attractions that the north-west has to offer. You'd think he'd be proud to have a spanking new art gallery. But what does he do? Tries to put people off with negative comments.'

Auntie Annie didn't say anything.

'You know, Annie, each time I come back to Merseyside I hear the same old smart-alecky comments. There's nothing they love better than a clever put-down. No wonder all the ocean liners went down south. People probably got tired of hearing the same old jokes.'

'Is that it?' asked Auntie Annie.

'Yes. Gosh, it's amazing what they've done with the old docks, isn't it? Do you remember how it was before?'

'Yes,' replied Auntie Annie. She had seen the warehouses that had been transformed into the Albert Dock complex every day for fifty years as she travelled, first to school, then to work, on the ferry boat.

Once inside, Harold guided Auntie Annie towards an exhibition on Modernism. They stopped in front of a picture that looked like a spider's web and Auntie Annie said it looked like a spider's web. 'What's it called, Harold? I haven't brought my glasses.'

'It's called Three Figures on a Plane,' Harold replied, stepping back to admire the picture.

'I can't see three figures. And I can't see a plane either.'

'It's abstract,' tried Harold, wishing that Auntie Annie would keep her voice down.

'I don't see the point of it myself,' said Auntie Annie. She looked around. 'They've turned part of the dock into some very cosy flats. My friend Kitty's been in one. She said it was really lovely. Double-glazed too. All very tasteful.'

'It's this way to the Giacomettis, Annie,' Harold said.

Auntie Annie surveyed the angular figures dispersed around the large room. They reminded her of rusty railings.

'There's something very old about them. They speak of prehistory. They're really totemic,' said Harold, doing a slow-motion little dance to take in the exhibits from every angle, allowing them to disappear from his sight, then turning to let them catch him by surprise with the boo of the shock of the new.

'They all look the same,' said Auntie Annie. Harold tried to blot her out and walked away. Auntie Annie followed him with her voice. 'They must be a bugger to dust.' She could see what Harold was up to. He was ashamed of her, of his roots; had gone away, only returning for a fleeting few days each year full of news of London and new friends and travels abroad. But, in between times, he forgot her and his old mum. 'I wouldn't give them house room,' she said, loudly enough for Harold, and everyone else in the room, to hear.

Harold looked around unhappily, took Auntie Annie's arm and led her towards the lift. 'They've got a special exhibition of the Japanese Avante-garde. I saw it previewed on "The Late Show".'

'Did you, indeed?' said Auntie Annie, who had only ever frowned in on 'The Late Show' en route to 'Cell Block H'.

'I'll pay. It's really very reasonable for a pound. In London it would be three times that.'

'Yes, well they probably give us a special rate 'cause we're so poor,' Auntie Annie said, thinking of four pints of milk.

They found themselves surrounded by huge canvases which showed a rather plain Japanese woman in pre-Raphaelite settings.

'I once got a birthday card with that on the front,' said Auntie Annie. 'Not with a Japanese face, though. Why have they just copied old paintings, Harold?'

'It could be an *hommage*, Annie. Mind you, there's something distinctly surreal about them too, don't you think?'

Auntie Annie looked at Harold. 'I'd like you to call me Auntie Annie, Harold. Like you used to.'

'Would you? All right then.'

'Thank you.'

'Mind you, they're not paintings at all. They're computer-assisted photographs.'

'Just snaps? Fancy!' said Auntie Annie. Why, she wondered,

was she talking like this? What had got into her? She felt she was beginning to sound quite common.

They moved into a darkened room where, on the floor, hundreds of digital displays in red were computing an infinite variety of seven-digit numbers for their edification and instruction.

Auntie Annie was silent. Harold approached her after walking round the display twice, frowning and thoughtful. 'What do you think?' he asked her.

She noted that he had not used Auntie yet. Also, he had dropped the Annie. 'It makes me think of Tesco's,' she said.

Harold said nothing. They walked on to the next gallery. Auntie Annie saw a large sign. She pretended she couldn't read it. She felt old. 'Read this for me, Harold.'

'"If you have any questions about the exhibits, ask the attendant",' said Harold.

'Now that's nice, isn't it?' said Auntie Annie. She concentrated on the notice, stepped back, approached it in a Harold-like manner, stroked her chin.

'Er . . . come this way. This is interesting.' Harold led Auntie Annie into another darkened area, where a bank of twenty-four identical television monitors graced each of the four walls. The monitors alternated between showing nothing, a single oriental eye and a palpitating open heart. A single monitor in the middle of the room asserted that the body had its mysteries.

'It's like watching "Your Life in their Hands" in Rumbelow's window,' said Auntie Annie.

Harold scowled. Annie's normally fairly refined Wirral voice was becoming the spitting image of the dreadful mother's in 'Bread'.

She looked at him. 'What does it say to you, Harold?' she asked. 'Explain it to me, please.'

'If a work of visual art could be explained in words there would be no point in making it visual. You have to experience it . . . er . . .'

Yes, he's definitely holding back the Auntie, she thought. He was a stubborn little tyke all right. Always had been. What he'd put his mother through . . . He'd had it easy. It was everyone else who'd had it hard.

'And they brought it all the way over from Japan, did they? I don't know what your dad would say if he'd lived. They're all Sunny tellies too. Your dad wouldn't have anything Jap in the house.'

'It's 1992!' said Harold.

'Your dad was never the same after Burma.'

'No. Let's get on. We've got the Maritime Museum to do still,' said Harold impatiently.

Auntie Annie looked at Harold's back as he made his way towards the final exhibit. A huge notice covered one wall, a notice large enough for Auntie Annie to read without glasses.

'THIS SENTENCE DOES NOT CONSIST OF EIGHT WORDS,' she read. 'One, two, three, four, five, six, seven, eight . . . But it does have eight words, Harold! It does. They've made a mistake.'

'No,' replied Harold. 'They've made a point. The artist is saying that things are not as they appear, that there are secret truths.'

Below the notice were three identical objects: eight-sided, covered in white tiles with gold-coloured dogs on top, together with a gold handle that read: LOVE/HATE; DAY/NIGHT; GOOD/BAD. Auntie Annie sat on one of the objects. She felt tired. *I think I understand*, she thought. *I think I now know how it is. We become old and the world becomes more and more peculiar. The older we get, the stranger everything and everyone gets. Until finally Death is a friend because it is at least easy to understand. As simple as a hole which the Co-op coffin fits just right.*

'Love! Don't sit on the exhibit, love! There's a pet!' said an approaching female attendant. She had friendly bubbly hair, like the woman at the pet-shop Auntie Annie frequented.

Auntie Annie stood up. 'What does it all mean?' she asked the attendant.

'Don't ask me, love. I'm the resident dick 'ead. The brainy bonce is off having 'is dinner.'

'Are there good places to eat at on Albert Dock?' asked Auntie Annie, happy to be led off on a familiar tangent.

'Between you and me, they're a bit pricey. Here at the gallery they'll charge you a couple of quid for some quiche,' said the attendant.

Harold came over. The attendant put a white glove on her right hand. 'Don't ask me what it means, love. I'll lift the lid for you, though.'

She lifted the heavy lid of the white octagonal object. Inside mirrors covered every surface. 'Stick your head in there,' she said to Harold.

Harold did as instructed.

'What can you see, Harold?' said Auntie Annie.

Harold could see that his jowls hung down; that the bald spot on the back of his head had doubled since he had last looked; that he was getting a double-chin at the back of his neck; that he was not the bright young man he felt himself to be most of the time. *I can see how it is, how it is going to be*, he thought.

'It's just some mirror. New Brighton fairground had a better one,' he said.

'The fairground's gone, more's the pity,' said the attendant. 'Covered in greensward.'

'And the New Brighton baths. They've gone too,' added Auntie Annie.

The attendant smiled at her. 'And the pier. They love the greensward round 'ere. Where our 'ouse was is covered in it.'

'Where was it?' asked Auntie Annie.

'Scotty Road.' They looked at one another understandingly. 'You have a go, love,' said the attendant to Auntie Annie.

With difficulty, Auntie Annie leaned over the yawning hole, holding the rim hard. She looked around. At first it seemed as if she was in the middle of the three-sectioned mirror in the spare bedroom at home, the room in which Mum had died. She could see the back of her head. The perm was lasting well. Then she saw Joe Hamilton, who had wanted to marry her and who had disappeared to Canada when she had refused him. He winked. *That's typical of you, Joe Hamilton!* Mum was next to him and smiled at her. She saw her retirement party at the office. All her friends – now dead – raised their glasses to her. Then every cat in her life came to the edge of the glass and nuzzled her reflections.

'I think we'd better be getting on,' said Harold, addressing Auntie Annie's bent-over body. He's still refusing to call me Auntie. *Well, let him. Let him go*, they told her.

'That was really nice. A treat,' Auntie Annie told the attendant. 'I saw all sorts of wonderful things.'

'Yeah, it's ace,' said the attendant.

'I thought it rather a waste of time,' said Harold.

After a silent lunch and a tour through the Maritime Museum Harold and Auntie Annie made their way towards the ferry boat back to Wirral. Harold was feeling relief, already seeing himself gunning his Volvo down the motorway towards London. They passed the car park attendant. 'Was I right or was I right?' he asked them.

Harold walked on, but Auntie Annie went up to the car park attendant and said, 'This sentence does not consist of eight words.' The man looked at Auntie Annie, lost for words for once in his life. Then Auntie Annie nodded to him and slipped him a wink, resolving to return to the Tate Gallery North once Harold was safely out of the way. She found herself already missing everyone in the mirrors.

Ms Clip Inspects Ofingi

Ms Molly Clip, the English language officer of the British Council in Xombooty, brought her rumbling Landrover to a halt by a notice at the side of the road. She reached into the glove compartment and found, under the gloves, her reading glasses. These she put on, carefully replacing her driving glasses and storing them in the case against the dust.

Thus correctly attired, she read the notice:

OFINGI CHURCHI BAPTISTI / OFINGI BAPTIST CHURCH

O su cric-cric sep ronto sia blunt.	If your knees are knocking, get into them.

'That simply can't be right. Surely one gets "on to" one's knees, doesn't one? If one does, that is.' A little bemused she returned to the Landrover, changed her glasses and felt content in the main because the notice had at least shown her that she was getting close to Ofingi.

This deduction was confirmed after half a bumpy mile, where a second notice graced the side of the dirt road. This one was large enough for Ms Clip to read without changing her glasses:

OFINGI TOP POT DRIVERS SHIDI
Ofingi shoots careful drivers

Ms Clip shook her head. 'Confusion over the use of prepositions one can fully understand and, under certain circumstances, have some sympathy with. Infuriatingly difficult little words. Foreign language learners do indubitably have a great deal of trouble with them. However, one finds it rather more difficult to understand, still less forgive, mistaking the verb "to welcome" for "to shoot", especially when the foreign language learners have a Native Speaker in their midst.' Before driving on, Ms Clip gave the notice one of her frowns.

She resolved to bring the matter to the attention of the volunteer, Peter Brigham. 'I shall say that he has allowed a linguistic dustbin to be placed on the front porch. First impressions are so important. Whether in Bexley or Ofingi, one must not let one's standards slip. That is what I shall tell him.'

Ahead a group of picturesque conical huts came into view. As the track curved towards them, Ms Clip saw over to the left a large asbestos bungalow of a kind she had seen many times before all over Porsellana. She made for it, stopped the Landrover, reached for her other glasses and approached the door of the bungalow. Pinned to it, a notice announced:

MINISTRY OF EDUCATION AND LARCENY
(Ofingi Coven)

Ms Clip gazed at the sign, wondering what it all meant, as the Landrover sighed and ticked nearby.

'I should have inspected Ofingi earlier,' said Ms Clip to herself.

That she had not visited the British volunteer in Ofingi during the two years he had been there was understandable. Not only did the village lie three hundred miles from the capital, Xombooty, it was three hundred miles along an unpaved road which had, until recently, been infested by the Oshunto tribe who were in open rebellion against the ruler of Porsellana, Dr Emmanuel Tabbi.

Despite all this, Ms Clip had, to her credit, on many occasions suggested an inspectorial visit but had been put off by the British Council Representative in Xombooty, who said,

'What would I tell London if one of my gals was sent back minus epidermis and goodness knows what else? At the very least they'd cut out those cultural visits that recharge our burnt-out expatriate batteries. No more dipsomaniac thespians reciting the Four Quartets and feeling up the houseboys. I appeal to you, dear Molly! Don't go to Ofingi. Not now. After they've finished slugging it out, but not now.'

This had been sufficient to persuade Ms Clip, whose zeal for the spread of the English Language was the stuff of legend, to postpone indefinitely her visit to Ofingi. She had left Peter Brigham to sweat out his tour sans inspection, calming her conscience by sending him back copies of the *Times Educational Supplement*. But these small gestures left her feeling rather like a mother who sends her son food parcels while he is away at boarding school but never visits him or takes him for the holidays.

The door of the asbestos bungalow suddenly opened. A large man dressed in a suit, shining as if made from fish scales, emerged, completely filling the space once occupied by the door.

The large man shook Ms Clip relentlessly by the hand and greeted her, saying, 'We have ways of making you talk in Ofingi, dear virgin.'

'We have ways of making you talk in Ofingi?' repeated Ms Clip, half to herself, in the hope that a repetition would help her make sense of it. It didn't, but it did produce a repetition of the athletic handshake and a deep laugh from the large man.

Deciding to ignore what could only be the momentary confusion of the foreign language learner when faced with a stressful piece of communication, Ms Clip said, 'I'm Ms Clip from the British Council in Xombooty. I'm happy to meet you.'

The man looked puzzled for a moment. Then he shrugged and replied, 'I'm knackered to make your replacement.'

'I'm knackered to make your replacement?' repeated Ms Clip in a state of nearly total cerebral paralysis.

'I also,' beamed the large man.

'And how are you?' asked Ms Clip without hope.

The large man replied that his life was a bowel of cherries. Then he hurried her into the asbestos bungalow, saying that the sun was 'as hot as a baboon's armpit and would castrate her if she was not extremely circumcised'.

'How true!' replied Ms Clip in a daze.

The large man gestured Ms Clip into the bungalow, saying, 'Please to view my lair?' a usage which did little to set her mind at rest.

Once inside, the decor surprised Ms Clip somewhat. The place was the usual mess she had come to expect at Ministry of Education offices up and down Porsellana. What amazed her was the huge perspex and stainless steel desk which graced the centre of the room, behind which the large man sat down in a chair which brought 'Mastermind' to mind. For a split second the cosy sanity of a Sunday night in Bexley came to Ms Clip. 'Songs of Praise', 'The World About Us', 'Mastermind' – all accompanied by carpet slippers and a parade of hot sweet drinks.

She settled herself down in the chair across the desk from the large man. An ornate plaque, set on the desk dividing them, announced: Rev Dr Dunstan Minnie, Chief Thug.

'Dr Minnie, I have come to see Mr Brigham,' began Ms Clip.

Dr Minnie opened a silver cigarette box. 'Fag?' he asked.

'I don't,' replied Ms Clip.

Dr Minnie looked extremely disappointed. He reached into a deep drawer in the desk, producing a bottle of TabbiCola. This he opened with his teeth and passed to Ms Clip.

She drank and smiled and frowned.

'Tepid tears, isn't it not?'

She chose to ignore the remark. 'Well,' she said. 'To business. Thank you for the TabbiCola. I was very thirsty after my trip.'

'I am the chief thug of the office of Education and Larceny. How can I do you in?' asked Dr Minnie, sitting very tall and proudly in his seat.

'I will just ignore it,' thought Ms Clip. 'What else can one do?' She gave Dr Minnie her 'Do your worst! The might of the British Council and the BBC World Service is behind me' look and asked, 'Mr Brigham. Can you take me to see Mr Brigham?'

'He's up to no good in the woodshed,' replied Dr Minnie.

'Well, perhaps when I have finished this beverage,' asserted Ms Clip, in the voice that had made her the cause of fear and bed-wetting among Libyan students at The Quick School of Languages where she had commenced her illustrious career, 'you will escort me to the er . . . woodshed.'

'You're shot,' said Dr Minnie amiably.

The school consisted of five tents. As Ms Clip and Dr Minnie approached they could hear the sound of children chanting.

'And what is your appendage?' asked Dr Minnie as they walked. 'I ask because I must interbreed you with the hitmen of the woodshed.'

Ms Clip stretched her lips horizontally towards the apparition of unreason that Dr Minnie was becoming to her. But she said nothing and concentrated on picking her way across the uneven ground, keeping her attention focused on her Clarks Polyveldt shoes. They had been bought two summers ago in London. She had hiked in the Lake District in them. She had stayed with Lady Withers at her country house in them. They were the only things that made any sense to her now. She would have to have a long talk with Peter Brigham. That was certain.

She was shown into a large, smoke-filled tent. Five men stood and surveyed her, Ms Clip thought, as if she were a prize heifer. Then they greeted her in unison, 'Shoot to our woodshed, O Virgin!'

'I am Ms Clip of the British Council in Xombooty.'

They did not seem to understand her, however.

Ms Clip continued, 'I realise that it has taken me a long time to visit Ofingi but now I am here I would like to see Mr Brigham.'

The group of men looked at one another.

'We do not eat your pearls,' one of them said.

'You do not eat my pearls?'

'That's far right. Your pearls are over our turnips.'

Ms Clip could take no more.

'Mr Brigham! Take me to Mr Brigham at once!'

'The Lord Brigham is churning out sausages yonder,' said the spokesman. He held open the tent flap for Ms Clip to walk through.

Suddenly very tired, Ms Clip followed the man down the line of tents. From the last tent on the right she heard, 'And what's Sino doing?'

'He's sailing his boat on the river.'

'What can you see in the middle of the river?'

'An island.'

'What's on the island?'

'Trees, a house and a beach.'

'Who lives in the house?'

The class stood up as Ms Clip entered. 'Good morning, Miss!' They chorused.

She gestured the class to sit down and then turned to the frail, bespectacled teacher who stood next to a beautifully painted picture on a torn white sheet showing a boy sailing his boat on a river that had an island in the middle on which stood a house and trees, and said, 'I'm Ms Clip from the British Council in Xombooty. You must be Mr

Brigham. I do not wish to interrupt your class. Please continue.'

'Now we'll see!' thought Ms Clip.

But in that Ms Clip was to be disappointed. She watched a wonderful class which practised verb tenses, based on the startlingly beautiful picture on the torn sheet. The children were happy and amused. They spoke well; better, in fact, than any other class she had encountered in Porsellana.

When Peter Brigham had dismissed the class, he took off his glasses and wiped the sweat from his face. 'The game's up, I suppose,' he said.

Ms Clip said nothing.

Peter Brigham sighed. Then he said, 'You see, when I first came here, they, Minnie and his cohorts, treated me abominably. They refused me housing. I still live in a tent. When the kids' textbooks arrived, they took them and sold them to traders from the next island. Ditto the dried milk from the government that was airlifted in. I've had nothing to use with my classes, except what I've been able to make. Yet Dr Minnie has a storeroom stuffed with useful stuff. He's got the key. It's his. To distribute anything from that storeroom would lessen his possessions and make him the poorer. He can't face that. Then, when it was announced that Tabbi's hearts and minds programme was going to give officials from here first go at all the plum jobs, scholarships abroad and the like, they forced me to teach them English in the evening. English, they know, is the way to the big time. You can open a Swiss bank account if you speak English . . . get a job with the UN . . . wheel and deal in a really big way. Well, I started teaching them and I thought, "I'll show 'em!" And I have, haven't I?'

'Yes, you have indeed,' said Ms Clip. 'But you haven't taught this er . . . idiosyncratic language to the children?'

'No. The children are – ' and he shrugged ' – the children.'

Ms Clip smiled benignly at the volunteer. 'Well, I've

brought you some books for the children. With regards the others, I shouldn't worry about it too much if I were you. Seems to me that the buggers deserved it.'

The Consolation Bridges Bring

Standing at a bus-stop within sight of the Golden Gate bridge; staring down at a crushed aluminium can in the gutter; feeling the afternoon fog dampening him and waking arthritic pains in his knee and hip joints; expecting the bus to arrive at any minute but fearing it would not . . . Abraham Morgenstern addressed himself:

'My God, how you hate waiting in line! Hell for you is waiting in line.'

It was not that Abraham Morgenstern was impatient – Time and Trouble had bored that vice out of him – it was more that waiting in line jogged memories. Lines gave time for images of long lines long-gone long ago to develop in his brain like a Polaroid print, until the picture stood out with all the angular shine and sharpness of fresh barbed wire.

He tried to distract himself by shifting his weight from one foot to the other; by looking up and over the trees to where the bridge stood, almost completely enveloped in Pacific fog. A tiny section of the San Francisco tower stood out as orange-pink as a setting sun. Nearer, the Marin tower was completely hidden by the fog, though the suspension cable leading to it could be quite clearly discerned and from that distance looked like banisters for an invisible staircase to heaven.

The Golden Gate bridge usually consoled Abraham Morgenstern. Indeed, it had consoled him today. He had walked across it to Marin and down to Sauselito for a pistachio ice-cream on the wharf. Only coming back to the San Francisco side had the fog started rolling in to depress him. He had suddenly felt very tired as he joined the line of people waiting for the bus back to the city.

'You did a good job, Joseph Strauss!' he told the soul of the dead engineer who had been responsible for the bridge, who had believed that it was possible to span the Golden Gate, who had fought all opposition, supervised the building at every stage and had lived just long enough to walk across his work and nod with satisfaction at the great span that had flowed from his fingers.

'When you were fixing that last solid gold rivet to your bridge in March 1937, I had been arrested and was waiting in line for the train.'

A Porsche passed the bus-stop banging out a look-at-me chord from 'The Ride of the Valkyries'. Abraham Morgenstern scowled at the disappearing car but then, as it disappeared, he forgot that he had ever seen it. At once he was back in the crystal-clear memory lines in another country.

Lines for the train leading to unknown dreaded destinations; lines for the latrines; lines for strip-searches; lines, endless lines, for the ovens where smoke rose from the chimney day and night like fog – the one line he had, by fair means and foul, avoided, but the one line that memory had brought bubbling up to the surface of his consciousness on every single day since the first day he had witnessed it.

And that first time of asking, 'What are they lining up like that for?' and being answered by a wide-eyed look that contained all the horror waiting at the head of the line – that first time, perhaps, the Master Engineer, Joseph Strauss, had come, pipe in mouth, to look at his achievement, a bridge that bridged what everyone said was unbridgeable and bridged the chasm with beauty – a utilitarian sculpture to change men's lives, make them easier and happier; and, at the same time, complete the two headlands and the waters between, blessed to be joined by Joseph Strauss' Rainbow.

'You were a lucky man, Joseph Strauss,' Abraham Morgenstern told the sky above the fog.

*

At last the bus arrived. The line broke. It broke from the back. Some kids rushed forward in front of Abraham Morgenstern and, trailing laughter and the excretions of a ghetto-blaster in their wake, were aboard.

He waited. He knew his place. He also knew that he must not fall. To fall at his age might mean not getting up again. Anyway, lines always fell apart, he told himself. In the Camps they were dissolved by people pushing through, people fainting out of them; people breaking ranks to run headlong for the wire. Of course there were unwritten rules to the conduct of lines. Lines had their own morality. But if the aim of the line was attractive enough, nothing would hold it together. Lines, a rational invention surely, were the first casualty to man's warring emotions and desires.

He showed his Senior Citizens' bus pass to the driver, who did not look at it, seemingly taken up with the inaudible sound coming from the headphones attached to his Walkman. The bus was almost full. The kids had taken the last two rows and were shouting to one another raucously. The other passengers gazed hard out of the windows as Abraham Morgenstern unsteadily made his way down the aisle, looking for a neutral corner.

He spied a half-empty seat, half-filled by the fat thighs of a worn blonde woman. Her face as it glanced up at him seemed to say, 'I dare you to ask me to move over! I *dare* you!'

'This seat taken?' he asked her, his still-thick German accent placatory, gentle.

By way of reply the woman adjusted herself, thereby exposing a neatly penned DEATH TO PIGS! on the hard plastic seat. He looked at the words, shook his head and sat down on the seat with a long, tired sigh.

The bus lurched along Park Praesidio towards Fisherman's Wharf and downtown San Francisco. Abraham Morgenstern allowed himself the pleasure of anticipating the meal that lay ahead at the Tick-Tock Cafe. Would he have sole or lash out on the steak?

Then that thought disappeared too and he was watching the blue bay pass by on his left. Hundreds of small sailing boats bobbed up and down in the swell. Turning back, the shape of the Golden Gate was emerging from the fog; the sun, a dull yellow ball, edging towards it, preparatory to setting directly behind the bridge.

'Mr Strauss,' he told the dead engineer, 'I believe that the sun itself would move in order to set behind your bridge. Truly, my dear, dead friend, it steals glory from your handiwork.'

Then he turned away from the bridge and concentrated on anticipating dinner. He would have the steak and talk to his friends about the old days, when he had seemed to be at the front of every one of life's lines. Before the Bridge . . . before the war . . .

The kids at the back continued to shout and had turned up the volume of their ghetto-blaster. There was nothing unusual in that. The old man hated the sound and the idea of people being able to get away with such behaviour, causing distress to others with impunity. But he did nothing. Nobody ever did anything. He just sat staring at the graffiti on the back of the seat in front of him.

There was neither wit nor any redeeming features to such graffiti. He wondered, as he had so often wondered, what it all meant. What made these people go to the trouble of writing such trash? Who did they hope to reach? The unfeeling music from the back of the bus and the graffiti seemed to him to be part of the same thing: the barbarians are at the gates. Where had he read that? It was from a poem he had once known by heart. No, the name escaped him. Only the line and the realisation of the truth of it remained with him.

Where was he? Ah, yes. They were passing Fisherman's Wharf. Soon it would be time for Abraham Morgenstern to catch a glimpse of the mural. There were many painted on the walls of buildings in San Francisco, but the one coming up was his favourite. It showed a Hispanic couple, radiant and golden, carrying a lamp. Behind them a procession of people from all over the world – a line of the worldwide tribe of 'folk' – marched, singing and smiling. The mural seemed to him to speak eloquently for what America on its back-slapping, better days could be: of the America that had welcomed him, emaciated and shattered, with a Statue of Promises, and that other great bridge. That other bridge, the Brooklyn Bridge, had been lit up like a wedding arch when his ship passed under it. What joy he had felt. How consoling bridges were! America's great bridges bound the continent like a mother's hands her child.

The bus stopped next to the mural. He smiled at its primary colours. He felt his hand itching to rise and wave at the people in the mural. But then the hand clenched as he saw that someone had written in spray paint across the two beautiful faces leading the line: LIFE IS NOT THIS BEAUTIFUL!

The old man closed his eyes. On cue, the old memories returned to pester him. Graffiti had been written on him. He could turn up the frayed end of his shirt sleeve and see the graffiti: MORGENSTERN 6394245. And he, in his turn, had tried to immortalise himself in graffiti; to write his name and number in the corner of the hut so that some day someone would know that he had been there, had existed.

'Strauss, my friend!' exclaimed Abraham Morgenstern. 'Such a memorial you made for yourself!'

The bus left the mural behind. No, life was not beautiful, but why say so? Maybe the mural could have sparked hearts and improved things. Who knows? The man who had written over the mural had simply managed to spread ugliness and despair a little further than was necessary – to daub a minus where there had been carved a plus. Had not a man taken a hammer to Michelangelo's *Pieta*? It was the same. The barbarian is at the gates? No, thought Abraham Morgenstern, the barbarian stalks our streets. The barbarian is in the city.

Suddenly he was startled out of his reveries by a young woman. She turned in her seat and shouted to the kids at the back, 'Do you think you could turn the volume down? It's very annoying for the passengers.'

She said it quite calmly, though the old man thought he detected a nervous tremor in her voice.

Abraham Morgenstern did not look round. He did not touch the woman on the shoulder to compliment her on her courage. He did not add his voice to hers. All these things he desperately wanted to do. His whole body ached with empathy towards the woman, but he could not bring himself to do anything. He was fearful of both embarrassment and reprisals. He merely sat very still.

'It's very annoying for the passengers!'

A cruel send-up of the woman's voice was shouted from the back.

Then the woman had turned and was addressing him. 'It's terrible the way they act. You can't even ride a bus in peace.'

He nodded his agreement and wondered if his nod would be interpreted as partisanship by the kids. He devoutly hoped not. Better a thousand times to let whatever was going to happen happen. Get off before your stop if necessary. But never, never interfere in any way. They would get you if you did. Best to blend in with the graffiti and the fear and the passing blur outside.

But another side of him protested. Another side would have done anything to avoid the anguish which now racked him. To sit there – TO SIT THERE – and do nothing. To be scared and old and impotent in the face of ignorant, strutting unreason! All the books, symphonies, experiences, sorrows, people-memories in his old bald head stood for nothing. They would never respect him. To them he was a thing. That was why they were barbarians. They could not put themselves in other people's shoes. Just that.

He was full of conflict. He was sweating and he was shivering. He desperately wanted to release his pain, to shout at the kids, 'Turn it off! Show some respect!'

But he sat on in his pain, his body clammy with nervous sweat, his heart beating faster than the junk music from the ghetto-blaster.

The kids were making remarks about the woman who had spoken out. When this did not produce any reaction, one of the kids, his hair shaved, black make-up around his eyes, came forward along the aisle, an unlit cigarette between his lips. Abraham Morgenstern saw that he was wearing a tiny swastika earring.

'Got a light for my cigarette?' he asked the woman who had spoken out.

'I don't smoke,' replied the woman, her voice trembling.

'I wasn't asking if you smoked, I was asking if you had a light,' replied the kid, looking back towards his companions, a sneer on his face.

'The sign up there says you shouldn't smoke. You can read, I suppose?' said the woman.

Abraham Morgenstern blinked. He knew that the woman had made another mistake but loved her for having made it, commended her to Joseph Strauss for her guts and her swagger and her civilisation. There had been a few in the Camps like this woman. They had not survived.

A voice came from the back of the bus. 'Ask her who's gonna stop us!'

The woman stood up and stared hard at the kid. 'Nobody should have to stop you! Nobody should have to! You should respect the space of others.'

The kid seemed intimidated by the woman's stare. He looked away, then back to his companions. They were silent and he knew that he had to do something or their scorn would be aimed at him.

He turned back towards the woman and spat at her. The

woman screamed and sat down, rubbing at her face with both arms.

Abraham Morgenstern sat on, knowing what he ought to do, knowing what Joseph Strauss would have done. But he had known what he ought to have done many times on this same bus route when others had done similar things and interfered with passengers. But, suddenly, here and now, he was very sick of himself and his silence; of his behind, passive on the plastic seat. Self-loathing arose in him, sufficient to snuff out fear.

Abraham Morgenstern stood up.

He faced the grinning youth. Looking into the kid's face, he thought he saw everything that had caused him pain in his life. He stared into the grey eyes of the kid and saw Unreason.

He hated what he saw and slapped out at the face, a gentle slap, exploratory almost, to make sure that the face was, in fact, there. The slap made a satisfying sound. He gathered his hands painfully into fists and banged them into the face and as he banged he saw blood and shouted, 'You monster! You evil little monster!' And his words changed into Hebrew and a string of ancient curses bubbled from his mouth.

The driver, finally forced to admit that something was not quite right on his bus, removed his stereo headset and called out, 'What's goin' on?'

But by this time the kids at the back of the bus had raced up the aisle and thrown Abraham Morgenstern to the floor of the bus where they kicked him in the face and body over and over again – to the accompaniment of the woman's screams and cries for help and the unbelievably noisy silence of the other thirty passengers.

Then, when the driver stopped, the kids pushed open the door of the bus, leaving Abraham Morgenstern with five minutes of unconsciousness before his heart stopped and his soul, first in line, was welcomed through the Golden Gate by his hero, Joseph Strauss – while the kids ran away into the streets of the city named in honour of the gentle Saint Francis.

The Punishment of Luxury

The Dark Green government demanded that extensive coverage be given to the first execution of a citizen convicted under the new transportation act. Broadcasting equipment was brought to Trafalgar Square by bicycle, tricycle and solar-powered scooter, and set up around Vehicle Compacter Number One, to the south of Sperm Whale Column.

A crowd gathered from early morning. Around eight, six Dark Green Ecological Enforcers pushed a black Jaguar into the square. Its owner, the condemned man, Dr Robert Stone of Cattawade, Essex, had been arrested, convicted and was now about to be executed for being found in possession of an automobile. This crime would have been sufficient to ensure that the doctor spent the rest of his natural life in uncomfortably natural surroundings, but what had brought down the full rigours of the new law upon his head was that he'd actually been caught *driving* his car.

The unfortunate Dr Stone had been spotted indulging in this unnatural practice by a Dark Green Reformer while re-forming ex-driving instructors on a piece of forestry land adjacent to the doctor's property. The Reformer had been trekking with his charges through this wilderness, pointing out the ravages wrought by acid rain on the trees. The disgraced prisoners – many in tears, their ancient car-coats hanging in tatters from their wasted frames – were kissing the trunks of damaged trees, begging forgiveness of The Wisdom and Spirit of the Universe as they did so. The Dark Green Reformer had been about to sing a verse of his favourite song,

'A Tree is Worth a Hundred People', when he'd smelled something unpleasant.

'Surely not . . .' he thought, and launched into the first verse. But then he'd stopped and sniffed again. He looked up into the trees where baby cuckoos were throwing baby blackbirds out of nests as nature intended. He inhaled again. The smell took him back more than a decade, and he saw himself riding through Central London in the gutter on his old Raleigh, looking out for glass, cursing the cars, smelling that smell. Then he saw the old Jaguar, with Dr Stone sitting furtively behind the wheel, moving along the drive nearby.

Dr Stone had been arrested, chained and brought to the Old Bailey in a police rickshaw.

The Jaguar was placed next to the compacter. The doctor sat in it stoically as the Ecological Enforcers pushed the vehicle into the machine. The public executioner flicked the switch. The compacter rumbled into life. The peace of rush-hour London was shattered. Goat-hands had trouble controlling their herds on the Whitehall allotments. Shire ponies shied. Thousands of pigeons, unused to a mechanical sound, took to the air in panic, wheeling and flapping. Even the ripening wheat in Kensington Gardens seemed to tremble. The doomed doctor looked up and caught sight of the steeple of St Martin's with birds soaring all around it. Then he saw the passenger door to his left coming towards him, the roof of the car crumple, approaching and retreating.

Five minutes later, the compacter opened its jaws to reveal a solid black and grey cube. This was manhandled to a corner of Trafalgar Square and placed on a plinth directly opposite The National Gallery of Batik. A sign was placed below the compacted Jaguar and Doctor Stone, which read:

THE PUNISHMENT OF LUXURY

That evening Arnold Watney watched news of the execution on the solar-powered green-and-grey television in Wolverhampton, set up on the street between the Jolly Miller Fruit Juice Pub and the Rude Health You-Bag-It store. He shook, thinking of Mabel the Morris Minor hidden under a sheet in his lounge at home. The crowd watching the television around him cheered and whooped as the compacter began its work. The cameras strafed the crowd. To the accompaniment of 'Ode to Joy', children with perfect teeth waved Dark Green flags and chewed on Nuttifroot bars; and housewives in handloom clothing shouted abuse at the sorely pressed doctor, saying that crushing was too good for him.

Arnold Watney, feeling guilty, tried to smell himself. He hoped that the peppermint leaves he had been chewing for the last half hour would disguise the tobacco, the home-brew beer and the car-wax – any one of which would merit a serious charge against him. Under the Dark Greens, the nose had become an instrument of great sensitivity. No longer anaesthetised by tobacco, car fumes, and alcohol, it had won out over the eyes and ears of the state and was able to sniff out all manner of iniquity.

Arnold Watney fled from his compatriots, wondering what he should do. He wandered into the Freedom Allotments that covered the whole of what had been the industrial area of Wolverhampton. He walked down the manicured paths kept shipshape by men with 'Convicted Smoker' printed on their uniforms. He walked past the Rottweiler Sanctuary. He could hear the chirping of birds, but behind that sound nothing disturbed the peace. Depression covered him like an illegal fishing-net.

Not for the first time he felt a deep desire to close the curtains in his lounge, uncover Mabel the Morris Minor, sit behind her leather-covered steering wheel, light a cigarette and pretend to drive her, whispering 'Vruuum! Vruuum!' between his teeth. But that was not possible. That would never be possible again. Why, oh why, he wondered, hadn't he got rid of all the incriminating things in his life when it had been easy. But he knew why. He'd been hoping the Dark Green party would be beaten in the election and the Light Greens returned. In retrospect, the Light Green Administration seemed like halcyon days to him. They had tolerated the use of cars one day a week. They had allowed one to smoke herbal mixture. It was even to be bought – though at a considerable price – at the larger branches of Rude Health You-Bag-It stores nationwide.

But the Dark Greens had cancelled elections until the world was once again clean. The cleanliness meant the eradication of dirty freedoms. Arnold Watney's panic rose. He was a dead man. At any moment the full weight of the Dark Green Revolutionary Cadre could sweep down on his house and take him away to share poor, crushed Dr Stone's fate. His only hope, he felt, was to confess his wicked addictions to the Dark Green Cell at the Tofunutri Processing Co-operative, his place of employment. They might send him off for weekend re-education, or, if they thought his case severe enough, give him a sabbatical at the Dark Green Re-education Centre in Mid-Wales. He shuddered. He had heard tales of what happened there. One had to dust the leaves of trees day after day, clean out badger sets, nurse cows in the Mad Cow Home, all the time reciting apologetic mantras to Mother Nature.

But even to embark on this dire course of action he would have to rid himself of Mabel the Morris Minor, the home-brew buckets, the tobacco plants, everything that made his pathetic life worth living.

Might it not be better then to die?

In bed that night Arnold Watney tossed and turned. He had more or less decided that life had to be better than the alternative, but the idea of parting with Mabel filled him with sadness, a sadness he was not sure he would ever recover from. Perhaps he would get over his addiction to tobacco and home-brew, but Mabel was his life. Still, at half past one in the morning he got up and went downstairs. By candlelight he began to take Mabel the Morris Minor to bits, weeping with every turn of the wrench.

It took him the best part of a fortnight to trundle small sections of Mabel out of his house at dead of night on the trolley pulled by his bicycle. He rode bits of his wicked but wonderful Morris Minor silently down the lane and dumped her with some ceremony into an ornamental lily pond. Each night he was certain that he would be caught by someone, but somehow his luck held. On the last night he took his home-brew buckets and added them to the pyre in the pond.

At last he was clean! Let the Dark Greens search high and low! They wouldn't find anything to pin on him! His heart, however, longed for Mabel. His lungs for a cigarette. His liver for a long cool pint of home-brew mild.

Arnold Watney confessed his deep cravings for uncleanliness to the Dark Green Cell at work. They shook their heads of herb-scented hair, and decided that he needed the *full* treatment. Arnold Watney joined a convoy of bicycles heading for Mid-Wales and the Re-education Centre.

He'd been dusting leaves, hugging trees and confessing his crimes to groups of fellow polluters for three weeks when news of the coup d'état reached them. The Dark Greens had been overthrown by a united coalition of Light Greens, Lilacs and The Pink Negative Population Party. Changes were being made. They were free!

He pedalled like mad back to Wolverhampton. Near Pembridge, Herefordshire, he passed some people digging up an old Volkswagen. In Warwick he saw a man with a fishing rod, wearing an accursed Walkman. When he arrived in Wolverhampton his neighbours, as bold as broccoli, were polishing their Ford Fiesta.

'I thought you'd got rid of that!' shouted a puffing Arnold Watney.

'We couldn't! We just couldn't!' confessed his neighbour, pulling on what looked suspiciously like a cigarette.

'Mabel! You've got to help me retrieve Mabel!' shouted the unreformed Arnold Watney.

An hour later, with the help of the neighbourhood, Arnold Watney was fishing Mabel the Morris Minor out of the lily pond. Things would be easier from now on. The grey-and-green televisions spoke of Glasnost and Perestroika. Words such as compromise and step-by-step fell on the nation's ears like the igniting of a match, or an engine, or the first tender pangs of desire. Arnold Watney gazed lovingly at the pieces of wet car as they emerged one by one from the pure water. He bowed down and kissed Mabel's bonnet, wiped the tears away from her back axle. And he knew that as he toiled to put Mabel back together again his life too would be back on the right road.

But the coup had only been a clever Dark Green government ploy to flush out cars and other hated objects from their hiding places, hypocrites from the concealed whited sepulchres of their desires. Two weeks later The Terror began in earnest. Up and down the country compacters crushed opposition without ceasing. And the Good Earth heaved a sigh of satisfaction on seeing Humankind put firmly – at long last – in its place.

Serving Suggestion

Though he knew he should have been thinking about something else, Mr Widdowson, watching the frozen carcasses of tuna slithering down the chute and along the conveyor belts towards the gaping entrance to the vat with its oscillating knives, was thinking of what the doctor had *not* said to him the day before.

'Do you want me to spell it out?' the doctor had said.

'There's no need, unless it's not serious. If it's not serious, you can spell it out – sing it out if you like,' Mr Widdowson had replied.

The doctor looked at his blotter.

'So there we are,' Mr Widdowson had told the doctor and was now telling the tuna as they passed stiffly by.

Half an hour later, Mr Widdowson was summoned by tannoy to the office of his boss.

'Any suggestions?' Mr Grant of Grant, Maley and Duff, canners of meats, fowl and seafood for over a century by appointment to the discerning, asked.

Mr Widdowson looked at the open tin of tuna in brine that had been placed in front of him, trying to move his nose – without being seen to be doing so – from the fishy fumes which rose up from the damp flakes of tuna.

'Well . . . umm . . .' he said.

'Yes?' asked Mr Grant.

'Well . . . umm . . .' repeated Mr Widdowson. 'I would suggest that we use the sea-blue lettering that shifted our soft cod roes so effectively. We should blow up the picture of the smiling tuna and on the back, just next to the computer price code, put the serving suggestion.'

'And how do you suggest we suggest serving it?' asked Mr Grant, a touch of terminal boredom in his voice.

'A pile of tuna next to a tomato, a piece of lettuce and a spring onion?' suggested Mr Widdowson.

As he spoke he looked up into the face of Mr Grant, a face which always reminded Mr Widdowson of a fully inflated red balloon with a moustache and horn-rimmed glasses. He could see that Mr Grant was readying himself not to be pleased. He tried not to care, and succeeded.

'It just won't do, Widdowson!' said Mr Grant, confirming Mr Widdowson's expectations in a most satisfactory manner. 'Our research shows that housewives are bored to death with unimaginative serving suggestions.'

Mr Widdowson felt like suggesting that they showed the flaked tuna being put straight into the bin, thereby avoiding all the dyspepsia and bicarbonate of soda involved in its passage through the human body, but he said nothing.

'Look what Fairoak Fishy Foods have done with their labelling,' said Mr Grant. 'A hologram showing leaping fish was truly inspirational. They sloughed off the past – and their Legionnaires'-Disease-in-their-Northern-Plant-scandal – in one masterly move. Children all over the country were demanding Fairoak Fishy Foods products and would not be put off by fear of a few bugs. On the other hand,' continued Mr Grant ominously, 'when I pass along the supermarket shelves and see our pathetic serving suggestions and those tatty tomatoes and bits of lettuce all over the plate, I curl up.'

'Well, I'll get my thinking cap on, Mr Grant,' said Mr Widdowson.

'Make sure you do. And the term is "brainstorming", if I'm not very much mistaken.'

'Right you are, Mr Grant. I'll get my brainstorming cap on,' said Mr Widdowson, trying to appear to please.

He left Mr Grant's office, counting the years he would have to survive at Grant, Maley and Duff, before he would qualify for early retirement. Then, realising that that was no longer an issue, wondered how long he had before the pain set in.

'Bad day?' asked Miss Fish in Quality Control through a haze of cigarette smoke.

'Par for the course,' answered Mr Widdowson. 'Grant's got a bee in his bonnet about updating the serving suggestion on the label of the tuna in brine.'

'I've never seen the point of serving suggestions, between you and I,' remarked Miss Fish, doodling a moustache on a smiling fish, the new trademark of Grant, Maley and Duff.

'Me neither,' replied Mr Widdowson. 'It just seems to be one of the givens that we have a plate on the tin and the product sitting on it in company with other comestibles that can be forced down on the same fork.'

'What's a comestible?' asked Miss Fish, all at sea.

'Why, shame on you. I would have thought that you of all people would know what a comestible was.' But Mr Widdowson did not go on to enlighten Miss Fish. Instead he observed, 'I expect serving suggestions originated when people couldn't read. A good clear picture showed illiterates what they were buying.'

'I just don't get on with tuna,' said Miss Fish, who, like Mr Widdowson, was not the world's greatest listener.

'Why?'

'Well, I can get it down part of the way, but it sticks in my craw somehow.' And she stubbed out her cigarette on an ashtray bearing the legend, 'Out of the Oceans and into the Can – that's the Grant, Maley and Duff guarantee to YOU!'

'Well, that's as may be,' said Mr Widdowson, as he often

did, 'but as regards serving suggestions, maybe they've had their day now that people can read.'

'You'd be surprised,' said Miss Fish.

'Of course, there's always the export market. Such as it is,' said Mr Widdowson.

'My Ari . . .' began Miss Fish.

Mr Widdowson raised an eyebrow but said nothing. Miss Fish was always talking about her Ari, but Mr Widdowson was of the opinion that her Ari was not strictly hers at all, but rather Mrs Leptos's Ari. Mrs Leptos had five nasty children with skateboards to prove he was hers, after all.

'My Ari,' repeated Miss Fish doggedly, 'thinks we should scrap the serving suggestion on the label and itemise all the good things that go into our tuna in brine.'

Mr Widdowson humphed and sat down to meditate on a can of Korean tuna in brine that had acquired forty-three per cent of the market in the six months it had been available. What, he wondered, did Je-Ju tuna in brine have over theirs? But his thoughts were interrupted by Miss Fish.

'My Ari says that people want to know what goes into the tins . . . apart from tuna and brine, that is.'

And Mr Widdowson saw a picture of Ari in his white coat and green wellies adding shovelfuls of white powders and pale blue pastes to the vast vat of churning tuna in brine in the processing plant down the corridor.

'My Ari says,' continued Miss Fish, 'that we need to counteract the negative impression left on the public psychy-yoyo-ology by the last case of food poisoning.'

'No, I think Aristotle is barking up the wrong tree there, Miss Fish,' replied Mr Widdowson knowingly. 'The public would not be in the least reassured by having chapter and verse about what Aristotle adds to the tuna in brine to help it past the tonsils. I think it is much better that we leave well alone. "Permitted Flavouring" will do nicely.'

'Ah, but will it?' asked Miss Fish in her Archimedes fresh-out-of-the-bath tone. 'Will it?'

'How do you mean?'

'What I mean is that the government is going to force us to come clean about all the additives we put in.'

'Is it?'

'I have the relevant documents in front of me as I speak!'

'Do you now?'

And Miss Fish rustled the relevant documents, though Mr Widdowson, still imagining he could smell tuna in brine, wondering if there would ever be a time when he would *not* smell tuna in brine – then, smiling sardonically with the realisation that there would, indeed, be a time – did not feel he could face the Government papers just at the moment. He did not take Miss Fish's bait. Instead he thought, uncharitably, 'If I were Aristotle, I'd throw Miss Fish back and do my best to please Mrs Leptos.'

But Mr Widdowson was not Aristotle. He was Mr Widdowson, married to Mrs Widdowson – with all that that entailed.

'I'm home, darling!' he called up the stairs, hoping against hope that Mrs Widdowson would be out.

'I know you are! I can smell you from here!' Mrs Widdowson called down.

'What's for dinner, ducky?' Mr Widdowson asked his wife as she came down the stairs spraying Floral Carbona at him.

'What day is it?' asked Mrs Widdowson.

'Tuesday, dear.'

'And what do we have on Tuesdays?'

'Three-pulse stew, sweetness.'

'Well, there you are then.'

'I was only trying to be sociable, honey.'

'Liar! You were trying to be *trying*!' replied Mrs Widdowson vehemently.

'I wasn't, flower. Honestly!' said Mr Widdowson, though, in reality, Mrs Widdowson was right.

Mrs Widdowson sniffed the air. 'You've been talking to that dreadful Fish woman, haven't you?'

'Well, petal, she is a colleague, after all!'

'She's an adulteress and a chain-smoker. I don't know which is worse. I've a good mind to send her your dry cleaning bills.'

'She'd plead poverty, pet,' observed Mr Widdowson, correctly. 'But tell me about your day, poppet.'

Mrs Widdowson ladled Three-pulse stew on to Mr Widdowson's plate. 'I licked stamps for "Save the Whale" in the morning and got Rolfed in the afternoon.'

'Rolfed, lovey?' asked Mr Widdowson.

'You wouldn't understand. It's a liberating form of massage.'

'Is it, treasure?'

Mrs Widdowson had commenced masticating her first forkful of Three-pulse stew fifty-six times, and therefore did not reply. On each chew she repeated a Sanskrit mantra.

Mr Widdowson took the opportunity to unburden himself about his problem with the labelling of the tuna in brine cans as Mrs Widdowson chewed.

After she had swallowed, she observed, 'Well, you know what I think.'

'What, heart?'

'I think you should leave that charnel house in which you work. It's throttling your spirit.'

'But how would we eat, precious?' asked Mr Widdowson.

Reply came there none. Mrs Widdowson had commenced chewing another forkful of her dinner.

Mr Widdowson got up early the following morning, leaving his wife sleeping. He usually got up early, because if he waited for his wife to rise, he would have to eat breakfast with her. Mr Widdowson could put up with most things in his married life but he could not stand seeing his wife at breakfast. Also, if he had his breakfast with her, he would have to eat grilled tofu.

The front door went click-clack as he closed it quietly and headed up the road.

At work, he sat at his desk in the silent Administration Building of Grant, Maley and Duff, looking at a can of tuna in brine. He had dreamed of tuna in brine during the night, but his dream had not enlightened him about what to place on the label instead of a serving suggestion.

'I'm losing my touch,' Mr Widdowson told himself. Then he corrected himself and smiled. 'I'm losing *touch*.'

At eight-thirty he mooned out of his office, chewing a pencil, and made his way down a dank corridor towards the Processing Plant.

He came to the tuna in brine vat and stood over it, looking in. He could see Aristotle, his back towards Mr Widdowson, sitting on a packing case, reading *The Daily Moon*.

Mr Widdowson did not say hello, but peered into the churning mass of tuna in brine. The swirling fish flesh was browner than remembered. Aristotle still had some way to go.

Then Mr Widdowson thought of the poster in the kitchen above the fridge at home. It showed dolphins jumping in a blue ocean. He had never taken much notice of it. It was just one of Mrs Widdowson's 'causes'. But, now, standing over the vat, he imagined the brown flesh coming together again and leaping out of the stainless steel container and flying, like the dolphins, over his head, out of the window, over London, down the Thames, along the Channel, across the Atlantic, and travelling South, always South, into warm, jumping seas. And Mr Widdowson saw himself riding on their backs. He looked at himself in the shine of the stainless steel vat and did not like what he saw at all. He was the wrong colour. His face had an amber patina. And things could only get worse.

'Let's go!' Mr Widdowson shouted to the fish flesh in the vats.

Aristotle turned, thinking he heard a shout above the churning of the machinery, and thought he saw a leg disappear into the entrance to the vat. He turned back to *The Moon*, reasoning that he had had one too many ouzos with Miss Fish the night before. Fifteen minutes later, he cast an expert eye over the vat of tuna in brine, thought it unusually dark, computed how many shovelfuls of his pastes and powders would be needed to bring it back to standard condition and went off to put on his green wellies.

Blow-Pipe

'The Little Bentley Sentinel', March 4th 1948

It is with great regret that we announce the death of Mr Cecil Puckeridge who passed away on Sunday last while tolling the great bell at St Cuthbert's. Mr Puckeridge – Cess to his many friends in the village – will long be remembered for his support of the Little Bentley Hunt, and his sterling work on behalf of the Territorial Army. He is survived by his un-married daughter, Agatha.

'The Little Bentley Sentinel', January 10th 1949

It was half past ten when we all gathered at Little Bentley railway station to bid farewell to Miss Agatha Puckeridge at the start of her journey to Borneo, where she will be working as a lay missionary to spread the Light of Truth among the wild people of that benighted island.

The vicar of St Cuthbert's told her that she would be in our prayers. I am sure all readers of 'The Sentinel' will devoutly second that motion.

Good Luck, Agatha Puckeridge! God speed!

'The Little Bentley Sentinel', May 12th 1949

Dear Editor,
I am writing to you because I am sure your readers would like

to hear some news regarding dear Agatha Puckeridge and her progress with the missions in Borneo. This week a letter arrived.

After a tiresome sea voyage, Agatha landed at the town of Kuching on the west coast of Borneo. Agatha was charmed by this town, which has a very large population of cats. She tells me that 'Kuching' actually means 'cat' in the local language. At Kuching Agatha rested a few days, and then embarked on a smaller ship for Kuala Baram, three hundred miles north-east along the coast, from whence she was taken by river steamer up the Baram river to Merudi.

It is from Merudi that she wrote the letter. There she is learning the language of the Penan tribe, naked jungle-dwellers who inhabit the area up-river from Merudi. I detected in her letter a certain trepidation at finding herself so far from home. At first, she says, she was afraid to go out on to the streets because of the near-naked tribesmen and their bare-breasted wives. It seemed such a long way from Little Bentley, she said. One interesting fact she mentions is that in Merudi the natives employ long hollow wooden tubes and blow darts from the end. One morning, she saw a man blow one of these darts into a dog. The dog stumbled along for a moment and then dropped down dead! Agatha said she was shocked at the sight, but knew she would have to come to terms with such barbarity, while hoping that she would be able to wean the people from this and other – unmentionable – barbaric practices.

Agatha asks for your prayers as she embarks on the final stage of her journey.

Madge Elmstead

'The Sentinel', November 30th 1949

Dear Mr Tendring,

I was very pleased to receive the copy of 'The Sentinel' in

which you had included dear Madge Elmstead's letter. I was also delighted that you should request a periodic letter from Borneo.

I have now been at the mission station of Mulu for a month. I am writing this during a fierce rainstorm. The heavy drops of rain plop on to my leaf roof. Some children and a dog have come to my little hut for shelter. The mission consists solely of myself, I'm afraid. Without the visits from the children I should be very lonely indeed.

I fear that so far I have not made any converts. Mulu is situated near the confluence of two rivers, the Baram and the Nagas. We are on the Baram, just a few hundred yards upstream from the place where the two rivers meet. Around the corner, on the bank of the Nagas, is a Catholic mission which has been here much longer than we have. I'm sorry to say that most of the Penan have already been swallowed up by the rapacious jaws of Popery. You see, the Catholic fathers came armed with rosaries, medals and holy pictures, while I have just five copies of the Book of Common Prayer. The people are simple. It is hard to tell them the obvious advantages of Anglicanism over the Roman Church. They fall in love with the baubles at once – all the things that we at St Cuthberts so frown on.

Last week I met the blow-pipe maker. He lives up-river from the mission. Reading Madge's letter to you, I see that she mentioned the incident in Merudi when a tribesman killed a dog with one of these contraptions. Watching the blow-pipe maker, whose name is Cantab, is an education. He is very amiable and a widower. He has not so far given way to Rome, and I have high hopes that he will be my first convert. Cantab makes the most wonderful blow-pipes with the crudest tools imaginable. When he has finished, one can look through the nine foot hole and see a perfect circle of daylight at the other end.

A blow-pipe is very easy to use. One takes a needle-thin

sliver of wood about nine inches in length and dips it into a poison. At one end of the dart, there is a round, spongy flight which fits snugly into the hole of the blow-pipe. Then, one aims the blow-pipe towards the quarry and blows hard. The dart flies out of the other end, completely silent, completely invisible, and – with luck – kills the victim. It is then possible to retrieve the dart, and reuse it.

Cantab's skin is a beautiful burnt-wheat brown. He is as lightly muscled and as perfectly proportioned as a Greek god. What a fine catch he would be for the Anglican Church!

I plan to build a little school here. Also a clinic, though I fear my medical skills are rather rudimentary. If we cannot win souls, then we can at least provide some help for the dear bodies of these gentle but surprising people.

Agatha Puckeridge

'The Sentinel', March 31st 1959

SALE-OF-WORK BREAKS ALL RECORDS

Last Saturday's Sale-of-Work in aid of the Cecil Puckeridge College in Mulu managed to collect £3000. This is a one-third increase on the amount raised last year, and represents an all-time record.

As all you avid readers of Dame Agatha's monthly *Letter from Borneo* will be aware, the money will go straight into the college's Scout and Guide Uniforms Fund.

'The Sentinel', January 30th 1969

Letter from Borneo by Dame Agatha Puckeridge
It is really hard to credit that I have been in Borneo for twenty years. So very much and so very little has been achieved in that time. The two greatest triumphs are our college and dispensary and we have the people of Little Bentley and elsewhere to thank for all your generous sup-

port over the years. Ever since 1962, when the last Catholic missionaries were killed by the blow-pipes of unknown assailants, our efforts at conversion have borne fruit. I am happy to report that few of the tribal people still cling to their old beliefs. It all seems a very long time ago when, led by Cantab – now of course our own dear Cuthbert – they joined the church in droves.

Several of you have written to me asking for news of Cuthbert, the blow-pipe maker. We are still fast friends and I am happy to report that he is in excellent health.

There is only one possible cloud on our horizon. The government keeps sending people to survey the forest and I worry that one day the loggers will arrive to attempt to tear down our Christian patch of Shangri-La. Cuthbert tells me not to worry, but I do worry . . .

'The Sentinel', July 6th 1981

FIGHTING ON GREEN DISRUPTS LITTLE BENTLEY–MULU SPONSORED HALF-MARATHON

Swarms of motor bikes tore into Little Bentley on Saturday and disrupted the start of the sponsored half-marathon in aid of the Lady Alresford Agricultural College in Mulu, Borneo. The unruly youths from other villages upset the tea-stand, pulled down bunting and shouted abuse at the adjudicators. The police arrived, but not before an altercation had started between the ruffians and patrons of the Puckeridge Arms. Three arrests were made.

'The Sentinel', March 9th 1985

Letter from Borneo by Dame Agatha Puckeridge
Well, after almost forty years in Borneo, it seems that all is not as 'civilised' as I had thought. Regular readers of these little letters will know that we have been waging holy war on

logging concerns for well over a decade now. It seems that
every time the loggers made a foray into the environs of
Mulu, a hitherto unknown group of Penans would attack
them with their blow-pipes, the darts of which are spiked
with a lethal poison. These periodic attacks had been
sufficient to frighten away the loggers. However, as the
whole of the lower Baram river becomes denuded of hardwood, the central government in Kuala Lumpur has been
licking its lips when it sees our still untouched little
Shangri-La on the map. Cuthbert warned me that one day
soldiers would be sent. I refused to believe it. Well, last
month it happened. A group of troops landed by helicopter
next to the hockey fields and commenced terrorising anyone
they could find. They pitched their tents on the hallowed
turf of our cricket pitch and went off into the jungle looking
for the tribes who had frightened away the loggers. They did
not return, and after a week Cuthbert and I went into the
jungle to look for them. Alas, all had been killed by blow-
pipe darts. The culprits had, as usual, melted away into the
jungle.

'The Sentinel', August 1st 1988

DAME AGATHA RETURNS TO LITTLE BENTLEY!

A throng of people turned out to welcome back to Little
Bentley the woman who has put us on the map while she
disappeared off it.

Asked about her reasons for her sudden return from
Borneo, Dame Agatha said that it was really the death of
Cuthbert, the blow-pipe maker, that had decided her to
leave. The Cecil Puckeridge College, the St Cuthbert Dis-
pensary, and the Lady Alresford Agricultural College in
Mulu are all in safe hands.

Dame Agatha is to take up residence at Green View
Cottage.

'The Sentinel', March 23rd 1989

CAN NO ONE STOP THESE VANDALS?

The spate of vandalism continues. Ten gravestones were found spray-painted with obscenities by the verger of St Cuthbert's on Sunday morning last; the two telephone kiosks outside Green View Cottage have also been rendered unusable; Mr and Mrs Thorrington, on their way back from Sunday service that same evening, were abused by a group of youths. Mr Thorrington was also assaulted and is recovering in the Lady Wivenhoe Memorial Hospital.

'The Sentinel', April 10th 1989

TWO BODIES FOUND IN LITTLE BENTLEY

Local residents of Little Bentley were shocked and horrified last Tuesday to discover the dead bodies of two youths during their early morning walk. The bodies were lying in the cemetery of St Cuthbert's. One of the corpses was found to be in possession of a can of spray paint. Police sources told 'The Sentinel' that forensic authorities have been unable to find any immediate cause for the deaths of the youths. However, the deaths bear an uncanny resemblance to the unexplained deaths of three youths in Colchester. They were struck down in the act of indecently assaulting a young girl outside a pub last month. Enquiries are continuing.

'The Sentinel', July 15th 1989

DAME AGATHA SETTLING DOWN HAPPILY

After all the frightening news we have had to report recently, it makes a pleasant change for your reporter to be able to visit our local celebrity, Dame Agatha Puckeridge. Doubly pleasant, because Dame Agatha was in fine form. We talked over tea in her comfy Laura Ashley sitting room. It was hard to imagine that this frail old lady had done such an amount of derring-do in her life.

Next to the copper bed warmer on the wall, I saw what looked like a spear. It did not fit comfortably with the rest of the furnishings. I asked Dame Agatha about it. She looked up fondly at the object. 'That's my blow-pipe, my only souvenir of Mulu,' she said. 'Dear Cuthbert gave it to me on his death bed. I keep it to remind me of him – and of all the good times we shared.'

'And are you settling down happily in Little Bentley after all those years away?' I asked her.

Dame Agatha smiled serenely. 'It has taken me some time to settle back in. But you'd expect that, wouldn't you? Still, I feel I am carving out a little niche for myself here in Little Bentley. There are always things to do to make oneself useful – just as there were in Mulu. One simply has to look for them.'

I left after tea, heartened and inspired by my visit to Dame Agatha Puckeridge. Truly it is consoling to know that an active little dynamo like Dame Agatha continues to lighten our darkness and lead us through these troubled times with her kindly light.

Long may she be a beacon to us!

The Age of Reason

At the age of seven it was thought that Benson had attained the age of reason. He was told by teachers and priests that he was now capable of telling right from wrong. Being thus able to discriminate, he was instructed rigorously in what to do when he erred. And what he was instructed to do was go to confession.

The nuns at the convent school, whence Benson dragged himself protesting daily, had taught him the formula for confessing his sins. He was to go into the dark little cubby-hole, kneel down, his face next to the grille, make the sign of the cross and then say, 'Bless me Father for I have sinned. It is one week since my last confession, Father.'

Next came the bad bits. The helpful nuns had given him a specimen list of possible lapses during rehearsals for the great day of his first confession. This list was rather like a serving suggestion on the label of a tin of vegetable salad. Because the nuns suggested 'I used naughty words three times, Father,' it did not mean that you had to say it. It was rather like the lettuce next to the dollop of vegetable salad. You didn't *have* to have a piece of lettuce. You could have a tomato next to the vegetable salad instead if you wanted. Still, the nuns felt that naughty words – and, if the truth be told, much else beside – went with seven-year-old catholic boys and girls.

During these rehearsals, the nuns had also suggested that while Benson and his contemporaries were waiting for their turn in the confessional, they should carefully examine their consciences, taking the ten commandments one by one and thinking carefully about whether they had given any a biff during the past week.

For a year Benson followed the nuns' suggestions religiously. Each Saturday evening he waited in line for his turn to come. While waiting, however, he was generally much too distracted to examine his conscience. Rather he was noting how long it was taking the grown-ups to come out of the confessional, and what terrible wrongs they must be guilty of to be made to kneel in the dark so long. Mrs Stone, for instance. Father kept Mrs Stone in for ages. Mrs Stone was always there when Benson made confession. In fact, it seemed to him as if Mrs Stone never left the church. She was as much a part of the place as the Our Lady of Lourdes statue to the right of the altar. It did not seem fair, therefore, that Mrs Stone be kept an inordinately long time in confession. When she came out she had to bear the looks aimed at her by curious queuing members of the Church Militant. What could she be telling Father that caused him to lecture her so severely, and at such length? He knew he did because he could hear the drone of Father's voice. Perhaps all her time in church was causing her to neglect her family and serve up unacceptable meals and not do the dishes with due attention and not make sure that all the wrinkles had been smoothed out of the bottom sheet when she made the bed and . . . yes, Benson could see that Mrs Stone might have large sins to confess. He found himself looking at her in a new, and not particularly complimentary, way.

But Benson didn't have anything heinous to confess to Father, behind whom sat Jesus and Mary crossing off Benson's sins like Mum crossed items off her shopping list. When it came to his turn he walked into the confessional as cool as Calvin, and rattled off Sister's suggestions.

'I used naughty words three times, Father; I was lazy four times, Father; I was disobedient one time, Father; I was greedy a whole lot of times, Father . . . those are all the sins I have to tell, Father.'

Father then gave Benson an easy penance. The worst he had got was five Hail Marys. He was in and out in a minute, not like Mrs Stone and some of the other adults whose verbose sins made him worry about missing Dan Dare on Radio Luxemburg.

Until one day a fortnight after his eighth birthday. He went in and told Father all the sins the nuns had suggested, following his usual custom. Now, whether Father had grown tired of hearing the same squeaky voice reciting the same old chestnuts week in week out and had decided to liven things up a bit, or whether he discerned that a more rigorous examination of conscience was way overdue, will never be known. Benson, waiting for speedy absolution, instead heard a long sigh from behind the purple curtain.

Father asked, 'Nothing else, young man?'

'Er . . .' said Benson.

'Does that mean yes or no?' enquired Father in a rather abrupt tone.

Benson had forgotten the original question. He didn't say anything for a long moment, a moment during which he thought of the queue outside wondering what he had been up to. Up to now Benson had taken great pride in being in and out in a flash.

'Yes,' he answered.

'So you *do* have something else to tell me, do you? I thought as much. Well, spit it out. It's a sin to conceal a sin in confession, you know.'

Benson knew. He worked his lips and frowned, furiously thinking of something to spit out. 'Er . . . I have uncharitable thoughts, Father,' he said.

'Yes?'

'Yes. When I'm waiting in line for confession, I think that the people who are in a long time must be really bad sinners, Father.'

'And what makes you think that?'

'I suppose it's the devil, Father.'

'Well, yes. The devil is behind everything that is bad in the world. But why do you think a person who is kept back in confession is guilty of serious sins?'

Benson didn't know the answer to that and just said er . . . Er . . . worked as well as more complex answers quite often.

'I'm keeping you longer than usual, aren't I?'

'Yes.'

'And you haven't committed any really serious sins, have you?'

'Er . . . no.'

'There you are then.'

'I had an uncharitable thought about you, Father,' added Benson, to whom it suddenly felt rather important to be hung for a mortal sheep rather than a venial lamb.

'And what was that uncharitable thought?'

'Well . . . er . . . I thought you might keep people in longer so that they'd be ashamed when they left and everyone in the queue looked at them, thinking uncharitable thoughts.'

Father sighed audibly, perhaps regretting that he had started this conversation in the first place. 'For your penance say . . .' And he launched into the words of absolution. He did it so fast that Benson had not finished his Act of Contrition by the time Father told him to go in peace.

Benson was standing up to leave, but then he realised that he had just had another uncharitable thought. He saw Mary turning over his new leaf and adding another black sin to the clean page, shaking her head sadly. Confession was supposed to give him a fresh start to the week, but here he was, his confession hardly over, and another sin already blotting his soul. He knelt down again. 'Bless me, Father, for I have sinned. It's just a mo ago since my last confession.'

'What do you mean?'

'Well, I had another uncharitable thought as you were reciting the words of absolution. I uncharitably thought that you were going too fast and not giving me enough time to say my Act of Contrition. The Sisters say that you mustn't just gabble prayers. They won't even get through the ceiling if you gabble them, let alone all the way to heaven. I thought you were gabbling.'

'Oh, you did, did you?'

'Yes, Father.'

'Beware of scruples, young man. That's scruples, s–c–r–u–p –l–e–s.' Then he added, rather brusquely Benson thought, 'Go in peace!'

'Thank, you, Father.'

Benson opened the door of the confessional and met ten pairs of eyes looking at him stonily. He held the door open politely for the next person and walked down the aisle to the front of the church to say his penance, very aware that the whole queue was thinking that he was a terrible sinner like Mrs Stone.

He looked up *scruple* in his Collins Gem. The meaning went over his head. But below *scruple* was *scrupulous* and it meant 'careful to avoid doing wrong'. That was easy to understand. It was the adjective. But what was wrong with it? Why should the priest tell him to beware of the noun? Benson felt strongly that the priest just didn't know the real meaning. It was good to be scrupulous, wasn't it?

That week he went around being scrupulous, so scrupulous that he wrote down all his lapses on a page ripped out of his jotter. On Tuesday, while passing the municipal tennis courts, he said 'bloody' to Carol, the girl he was forced to bring home from school every day because Carol's mum did not come home until late. He stopped there and then and wrote it down. Then he caught up with Carol, gave her a kick in the bottom, told her not to be so slow, that she was a soppy girl and was she aware that having to see her home every day was ruining his friendship with Peter O'Neill who said that social intercourse with girls was sissy; that Carol's mum had to work because her dad couldn't earn enough to keep the family. Benson's dad, on the other hand, earned more than enough to keep Benson in a manner to which he was accustomed. Then Benson said 'bloody' again in order to describe the state of Carol's house.

Carol stopped and started to cry, but she always did that. Had Benson not been able to bring tears to Carol's eyes – just as Bernadette had scraped at the ground and created a spring – the daily journey home with her would have been very boring indeed. He remembered the 'bloody', however, and wrote it down in his book.

Carol went on and on. Benson had had enough and sought to distract her. 'Let's go and tease Mrs Hangy-Out-Teeth.'

Carol dried her eyes. 'Bet you daren't!' she said.

''Course I do!'

'She'll chase you! She might even tell the park-keeper! Anyway, you won't dare! You always shout too quietly for her to hear. It's only me you're cruel to properly.'

Was Carol casting doubt on his manhood? 'You've seen how daft she looks. Almost as daft as you, Carol. I expect she'll burst into tears, that's what she'll do. All you girls are the same.'

'She's not a girl, she's a woman. She's old enough to be your mum!' said Carol.

Benson frowned. How dare Carol mention his mum! He walked off towards the court, where four women were playing doubles rather efficiently. One of the women had slightly protruding teeth. Benson could see them even when she did not smile, a truly unforgivable thing. He and Carol had often passed the group playing and Benson had made remarks to Carol as he swung against the netting of the tennis-courts.

'Go on then!' said Carol.

Benson made to kick her again. Carol moved away and just looked at him hard.

He was going to have to do it. The players were changing sides and Mrs Hangy-Out-Teeth was coming to their side. She was talking to her companion and collecting balls together, readying to serve.

'You're a coward!' shouted Carol in a most un-Carol-like fashion.

His lips had gone dry. Mrs Hangy-Out-Teeth was about to serve. He opened his mouth to shout, but nothing came out. He glanced over at Carol and she was giving him a look of the greatest contempt. The woman served. The ball banged into the net, making it shake. She threw another ball into the air and hit it. That ball went into the net too.

'Mrs Hangy-Out-Teeth! Mrs Hangy-Out-Teeth! Can't get a ball over the stupid net!' shouted Carol. Then she ran away at speed.

Benson was shocked to stone. Carol had taken the words right out of the back of his mind. He watched, appalled, as Mrs Hangy-Out-Teeth strode towards him. 'How rude!' she said. 'That was a very nasty and hurtful thing your friend shouted just then. I can't help the shape of my teeth just as you can't help being fat.'

'Well-built,' Benson corrected her.

'What's your friend's name? I'm going to tell her mother.'

'Carol,' replied Benson.

'And what's her address?'

'Er . . .'

'Come on, I haven't got all day! We hire these courts by the hour.'

'Fourteen Higson Street,' said Benson.

'Are you her brother?'

'No. I'm an only child.' Benson often told people he was an only child, especially in situations like the one he was now devoutly hoping he would soon wake up from. *An only child* sounded so lost and orphan-like, just a step up from confessing to being the Little Match Girl out of matches.

'Well, you tell that Carol that I'm going to talk to her mother,' said Mrs Hangy-Out-Teeth. She returned to the other three women, who were talking by the net and looking at him oddly.

He caught up with Carol by the sweet-shop. 'You beast!' he told her. 'You bloody beast!'

'Language!' said Carol.

They walked home in silence. At the gate to number fourteen, Carol asked Benson what he had told the woman.

'Nothing. I just gave her the wrong address. I said your name was Mary.' Then he fled to the safety of number twenty-two and stuffed himself full of toad-in-the-hole. He found it hard to get down and had not Mum been watching him like a hawk and talking about the poor children in China, he would have left it.

Full past his brim but feeling awful, Benson took his homework to the dining room which afforded a good view of Carol's house. Carol was, in fact, skipping innocently on her front path. He looked at her and shook his head. Carol had to be the world's worst skipper. She never got past three skips before the rope got all tangled up between her legs. Then she had to climb out of it, arrange the rope behind her heels and start again. Benson felt that he could outskip Carol – though skipping was considered an unmanly occupation – with one leg and one arm tied behind his back.

A grey Standard Vanguard came down the road and stopped outside Carol's house. Mrs Hangy-Out-Teeth got out. Benson watched appalled as Carol fled down the side passage of the house leaving her skipping rope a dead snake on the path. Mrs Hangy-Out-Teeth rang the doorbell. Carol's doorbell did not work, Benson knew. She waited. Then she banged the knocker. Benson's heart was in his mouth as he saw Carol's mother answer the door. The two women talked for a while, then he saw Carol's mother disappear. Carol appeared in floods of tears, the volume of which was Carol's special gift, spectacular enough to be put on display at the fun-fair. She was lectured by her mother as Mrs Hangy-Out-Teeth looked on. Then Carol was pulled roughly back into the house. Mrs Hangy-Out-Teeth walked down the road showing her teeth to the other occupants and drove off. Benson ducked down on the table, his nose against his composition exercise book, as the car passed. When he returned to the vertical he noticed that his nose had left a little grey mark on the page. He tried to erase it with his rubber but it only made matters worse. Sister would be angry. He shook his head as a truth struck him. Life was very certainly a vale of tears. It was as plain as the nose on your face.

There was a long queue for confession the following Saturday. Benson took his place at the end of the line, and started examining his conscience. *Thou shalt not have strange gods before Me.* No, he hadn't done that. *Thou shalt not take the name of the Lord thy God in vain.* No, he didn't think so. *Remember that thou keep holy the Sabbath Day.* Yes, he had remembered to. *Honour thy father and thy . . .* He glanced towards the door of the confessional. Whoever was in there was taking his time. It couldn't be Mrs Stone. She was three away from him along the row. Who was next to her? He pushed himself forward and saw Carol, her head bent over piously joined hands, holding a very effeminate string of rosary beads. He pulled back, worrying about what Carol would say. *Thou shalt not kill.* No, he hadn't done that, unless a bluebottle counted. *Thou shalt not commit adultery.* The Sisters hadn't even got up to adultery, so that wasn't included. *Thou shalt not steal.* No. He had taken a couple of scones from the tin in the pantry, but they were belongings of the family – held in common just like the early Christians – weren't they? *Thou shalt not bear false witness against thy neighbour.* No. *Thou shalt not covet thy neighbour's wife.* Defintely not. *Thou shalt not . . .* The confessional door opened and Mrs Hangy-Out-Teeth emerged, a black mantilla covering her hair. She held the door open for Mr O'Reilly. Benson hid his face in his hands prayerfully, and fretted.

What had Mrs Hangy-Out-Teeth said? He had not even known that she was a catholic. Had he known he would have been more careful. It was always better not to be a bully-boy on one's own door-step. He had broken a cardinal rule.

Deciding that he had better just recite the Sister's confession suggestions again, Benson gave over the rest of the eternity of waiting to worrying about what Mrs Hangy-Out-Teeth had said, and what Carol would say. She came out of the box in no time and, hands joined as if stuck with Gloy, her pearly rosary hanging down over her gym slip, wiggled down to the front of the church where she knelt devoutly in front of Our Lady of Lourdes – in full view of everyone – to say her penance. This she finished well before Mrs Stone was out, and started walking back up the church, giving sympathetic looks to the second seven stations of the cross as she went.

Benson felt that he would dearly love to give her a good kick in the pants. He would too once the hurdle of confession was over.

'I have used naughty words three times, Father. I was greedy twice, Father. I killed a bluebottle once, Father. I had uncharitable thoughts a whole lot of times, Father. Those are all the sins I have to tell, Father,' said Benson at speed.

'It's you, is it?' asked the priest.

'How do you mean?' Benson asked, shocked. He had been told that confession was anonymous. Priests had been martyred most gruesomely for preserving confidentiality. How dare Father!

'What I mean is that it is a sin to be cruel to little girls . . . and big girls too for that matter.'

'Is it?' asked Benson. It felt like the most natural thing in the world.

'To kick them in the bottom and make them cry. To tell tales . . .' Father went on.

Benson knelt, listening to his sin finding him out, wondering if he would be able to catch up with Carol on the way home and give her a real going over. It was obvious that she had spilt the beans. Had she had the gall to mention that he was going to come in three behind her? It looked as if she well might have. He would make her pay dearly.

Father gave him a decade of the rosary. Benson gabbled his Act of Contrition while Father gabbled the words of absolution. He left the confessional and almost ran out of the church in hot pursuit of Carol. He would say his penance before he went to sleep. In the meantime there was vengeance to be enacted on the wicked Carol who had committed the gravest of sins by trying to get her own back. Of course, he *had* told on Carol to Mrs Hangy-Out-Teeth, but she should have turned the other cheek like a Christian. He ran on after Carol until he got a stitch. At last he could see her in the distance, but he stopped running because Carol was walking hand in hand with Mrs Hangy-Out-Teeth. He trailed behind them. They disappeared into a sweet shop. Carol emerged unwrapping an ice-cream. This she licked happily, her spare hand in the forgiving hand of Mrs Hangy-Out-Teeth.

A bus passed Benson. He fumed. He hoped that the bus would mount the pavement as it passed Carol and Mrs Hangy-Out-Teeth. He closed his eyes and prayed that it would, but instead it just continued uneventfully along the wide road, on its way to the terminus.

Peter's Buddies

Dear Henry,

Do you remember that part in 'Tess of the D'Urbervilles' where Tess posts a letter and it gets hidden under a carpet and is not found until it is far too late? I have always been rather divided about that. On the one hand it seemed a trifle pat. Hardy made his whole plot turn on that unfortunate incident. But at the same time I know that it is the sort of thing that happens often enough. It's just that in the novel it did not have the ring of truth.

Well, I have to tell you that the exact same thing has happened to me. As the removers were sliding my hall cupboard on to castors during my move to Highgate, they found a letter. It was from Peter Thebus. I did not get round to reading it until this morning, and it has really taken the wind out of my sails. You will realise why when you read it.

Of course, I am kicking myself for not having been in touch with Peter. It must be at least a year. But he is one of many I have not contacted. These days I fear what I may find, if you understand. Peter's letter also made me feel unutterably sad, though you will probably agree with me that it is far from being a sad letter. But, more than anything else, I feel unhappy that I did not get in touch with him. It was not that I did not want to but, a day at a time, I postponed it. It all slips past so fast, you see, in such tiny amounts. And then suddenly there is no more time.

When you have read the letter, please destroy the copy I have sent you. A part of me feels rather guilty in sending it to you at all. However, I am taking the chance because I think that if anyone will know what has happened to Peter, you will.

All the best to you, Henry! Perhaps I shall be able to visit you again soon.

Sincerely,
Barry

New York City
14 December 1989

Dear Joel,

I received a rather strange letter from that literary Limey Barry Coe we got to know through Peter Thebus a few years ago. He was asking about Peter's whereabouts and enclosed the copy of a letter which he had received some time ago but which had gotten lost in a literary way that would appeal to Barry the Limey. I couldn't decide from his letter whether he was more interested in Peter or in telling me that he was acquainted with Thomas Hardy's novels.

I can't say I noticed anything odd about Peter when he passed through. I was his first stop. He arrived here about a week after he wrote the letter to Barry, stayed a week, did not eat me out of house and home, then was sent on to you. Are you still recovering from the visitation? Our dear brother Brits do seem to think that the colonies owe them extravagant hospitality when they visit our shores – must be a clause in the Marshall Plan with which I am unacquainted – and then treat us to a gallery seat for 'Cats' when we visit their rude country, staying like any self-respecting tourist, in an hotel.

Still, Peter does give good value. Being a New Yorker, I'd have thought that I would have instantly recognised the signs. I didn't. He was rather heavily made-up, of course. But one kind of expects that from someone who has trodden the boards for half a century.

Excuse the caustic tone. Three friends have succumbed in the last month and I am, as the saying goes, burnt out.

Is he still with you, Joel?

Always,

Henry

San Francisco

17 January 1990

Dear Saul,

I hate writing care of Post Restantes. I always think American Express drop such letters down the nearest refuse-chute. Still, there is no other way to communicate as far as I can see. If your itinerary has gone according to schedule then you should be arriving in Bali any time now.

I have just replied to an enquiry regarding your crewman, Peter Thebus. He has left a trail of anxious friends across Europe and the States, all wondering what has happened to him. Apparently they fear for his health. He seemed pretty robust to me – and to you, I should think – or you wouldn't have taken him on as a member of your crew. I am not sure whether I was more surprised that you were going to take him or that he wanted to go with you. I did not protest too much because, selfishly, I had feared he might be settling down with me to enjoy his crimson sunset years.

Anyway, I have passed all the intelligence I have about Peter back to his friends. I just hope you may be able to solve the mystery.

Sincerely,

Joel Parker

SS *Aqui Me Quedo*
Bali
Indonesia
12 February 1990

Dear Sister Margaret Mary Lim,

I am writing to thank you and all the other missionary sisters of St Rapunzel's convent, Solwezi, for taking in my friend Peter Thebus. I hope he has got over his pneumonia. I also enclose a money order which I hope will cover the costs incurred and leave something left over as a donation to the wonderful work you are doing at the clinic.

It had been my hope that somehow he would have made his way here to Bali and would be awaiting our arrival in port. After a week here there is no sign of him, and I must say I am a little anxious about him. I have been asked by his friends to report back but, failing any communication from you, I am unable to. A note about Peter's progress would be very much appreciated.

Thank you in advance.

Yours sincerely,
Saul Rosenbloom

St Rapunzel's Convent
Mintabo
Solwezi
Indonesia
1 March 1990

Dear Brother De Porres,

What has happened to that poor Englishman to whom you gave a lift that day when he was discharged from St Rapunzel's? The captain of the ship that brought him to Solwezi has written to me asking why he did not rejoin the ship in Bali.

As you will recall, I did not like to think of a man in Peter's condition going off up-country with you, but he was determined and, as you had a spare seat in the Landrover, and as he so wanted to move on, I did not see any point in objecting too strongly. Now I feel very guilty. Peter Thebus had but a tenuous hold on his life. He seemed set on risking it further, away from all friends and medicine. What has happened to the poor man? Please send your reply with the driver, if he has managed to reach you on the rough roads.

> Yours in Christ's Love,
> Sr Margaret Mary Lim

> Damien Leper Colony
> Port Cecil
> Solwezi
> Indonesia
> 25 March 1990

Dear Cousin,

Can you furnish me with news regarding our poor brother, Peter Thebus? Sister is worrying. You know how she is. Peter was her pet sparrow. Also mine. I must say that I was greatly encouraged in my work to see such a sick man able to give so much to our poor patients here. The cough he had was like none that I have ever heard from anyone in this tropical climate. I wish that he could have stayed on with us for, despite his terrible illness, he proved a godsend in our work. Many of our patients still ask about him. In a short three months' stay, he became beloved of all here.

When I consigned him to your care, I hoped that he would seek out medical help in Singapore. I thought that to be his only chance. He did not want to go, but I could not in all conscience allow him to stay. How is he faring, dear cousin?

Keep safe. The typhoon season approaches. Your little plane is such a fragile thing. But then we are all such fragile things, God help us.

> With loving greetings,
> Brother De Porres

Garuda Airlines
Singapore
7 May 1990

Dear Hok Wa Eng,

Do you remember the Englishman Mr Peter Thebus I left in your care at Kota Kinabalu? My cousin in Solwezi has written to ask what has happened to him. He had paid for a flight to Singapore, but during the enforced stopover in Sabah necessitated by Typhoon Maria, he came up to me in the hotel and said he wanted to stay on there.

He seemed to me too sick a man to stay anywhere that did not have a fully equipped hospital, but he was determined. Did he ever reach his mountain? If ever I saw Death on a man's face, I saw it on his. Still, perhaps I was wrong. Please inform me what happened.

Sincerely,
Sumano Sunton (pilot)

National Park Office
Mount Kinabalu
Sabah
Borneo
12 July 1990

Dear Mr Ambassador,

I have just received a letter asking for news about the poor Englishman who died after his ascent of Mount Kinabalu some weeks ago. His name was apparently Peter Thebus, not Peter Smith as he wrote in the park's Log book.

As you are aware, our guides did everything they could for him. They felt early on in the climb that he was too sick, but he would not be discouraged. He said that he wanted to reach the summit. It was all he wanted. They informed me that he died immediately. One minute he was standing looking out at the dawn from the summit of the mountain, then he was lying dead.

You are already in possession of all his personal effects. However, I would be grateful to hear of what has happened in this case as there seem to be other concerned people who are anxious for news.

      Respectfully,
        Hok Wa Eng (National Parks Officer)

           British Embassy
           Kuala Lumpur
           Malaysia
           23 September 1990

Dear Bill,

I have a bit of light to shed on the case of Peter Smith. He is (or was) apparently Peter Thebus, whose name rings a vague bell. Wasn't he once an actor of some repute?

You are in receipt of all his personal effects. I hope that my being able to supply you with a proper name for the deceased will help you to contact his next of kin. I am informed that he received a decent burial in the graveyard of St Mary's, Kota Kinabalu. I have the feeling that he died as he wished to die. He must have destroyed all identification prior to making the climb. We all face death in our own way, I suppose.

Case closed? Love to Fiona.

        Harry Moss

           Hampstead
           London
           1 August 1989

Dear Barry,

Goodbye, old friend. You will not see Peter Thebus again. This is my last stint in life's rep. I am going away and I may be gone – as Captain Oates remarked – for some time. You see, I have caught *it*. In a way I feel quite flattered that a man of my years could be struck down by a sexually transmitted disease. My one great fear is that the lesions now covering me will be mistaken for the Karposi Sarcoma that used only to afflict elderly Mediterranean gentlemen. IT IS NOT SO! I am no gentleman! I got it the newfangled way. I cannot recall the exact circumstances, but let there be no mistake about it!

I could of course stay put and be buddied to death. But I do not choose to. I had thought that I might go out on to the Heath at dead of night with a bottle of pills and ditto of Johnnie Walker, but am either not brave enough or not quite ready for the easy option. I've always been a bit of a travelling thespian. I see no reason to change now.

I intend to drop in on people to bid farewell, though I will not say anything about *it*. Perhaps on this final journey I may be able to do a few decent acts. I am very aware that my long life has been short on altruism – unless giving my all to the public can be considered as altruism. Also, as Death is a journey into the unknown, perhaps it is better that it finds me while I am embarked on one. A bit like Lear. Also, like Lear, I keep thinking, 'Thou shouldst not have been old, nuncle, until thou hadst first been wise.' Still, I am making a start. I have withdrawn all my money from the Halifax. I do not go gentle into that good night. Rather I go raging towards her screaming, 'Who? Me!'

Good night,

Peter Thebus

Supply Sides

It was Dr Trotter's first time outside Europe, and he had high hopes for the trip. He had to have high hopes. The words of the Chancellor of Goldsworthy College of Advanced Business Studies, which, as the Recruitment Brochure put it, was 'Set amidst the rolling countryside on the fringes of Workington and only a few minutes' ride from the bustling and historic town of Workington itself', still echoed in Dr Trotter's ears as he boarded the Porsellair jet and headed south.

'You're our last chance, Charlie! It's curtains for us if you don't manage to lure a couple of dozen rich Porsellanans to Goldsworthy. Your return ticket and expenses are scraping the very bottom of our seed-corn coffers. Don't fail us, Charlie! We'll be swallowed up by the Theme Park and Luddite Living History Centre up the road if you come back empty-handed.'

Dr Trotter, who had been saying, 'Who, me?' to himself ever since he had been chosen to be the single outrider for the Goldsworthy College Overseas Recruitment Drive, and who was more used to giving dry – though some thought them wet – lectures of a mildly disapproving nature on the subject of the History of the Multinational Corporation, had sat on the plane with his Taiwanese Leatherette briefcase open in front of him, reading and then rereading the brochure for Goldsworthy College of Advanced Business Studies. Dr Trotter barely recognised the institution described on the shiny pages of the brochure. It seemed like a strange and wonderful college – vibrant and yet somehow dreamy at the same time – of the sort he himself might dream about working in when days in the dim and dingy place that he actually knew as Goldsworthy College were getting to be too much for him.

As he read, hoping he looked like an Economist reader and representative of the new Thrusting Enterprise Culture, Dr Trotter refused the complimentary half-coconut filled with palm beer proffered to him by the smiling, bare-breasted Porsellanan flight attendants for which Porsellair was rightly world famous and because of whom the airline had come a close second in the category 'Most Talked About Airline' by the readers of *Up-and-Away* magazine, who had chosen the airline in answer to the question, 'Which airline provides you with the most post-flight conversation?'

Dr Trotter also refused to participate in the post-prandial Sky Spirits Dance held at the front of Economy. He had hardly looked up when the Flight Bursar emerged from the galley clad only in a black loin cloth emblazoned with the portrait of Dr Emmanuel Tabbi, the Father of Porsellanan Independence, beating the waist-tall Ongu drum. He had allowed himself to think how very different in ambience this flight was from his Danair flight to Jersey the previous summer, but, after one quick glance, had returned to studying his brochure, like a good businessman.

In the late afternoon the plane had plunged into Tabbitown Airport. At Immigration, Dr Trotter was relieved of his fountain pen by an immigration official, who said that a colleague had need of it in a back office because it might be a bomb. He had watched the pen, a gift from the Workington Women's Institute for a series of evening lectures entitled 'Whither the Corner Shop?', gleaming and glinting out of his life in the dark fist of the Porsellanan immigration official. Then, with a shrug, he had joined the other passengers to await the arrival of his luggage.

Half-an-hour later, bags started arriving. The bags were slung from the end of what looked to Dr Trotter like meat hooks, and then he realised that the revolving luggage conveyor was, in fact, the kind of mechanism one sees at Smithfield market when one takes students to see how their hamburgers arrive while the City sleeps. Also, his wife Gwen's best Antler suitcase, which she had made him promise not to let out of his sight for a moment, had not been placed on its hook by the handle – indeed the handle had disappeared – the hook having been rudely forced through its centre. It took him three revolutions of the conveyor belt to detach it. Airline officials laughed at him as if they thought it the greatest joke in the world. Dr Trotter aimed nervous smiles of disapproval at them.

Dr Trotter was not at his best when he was taken by the Cultural Attaché to the guest house dining room of the Isolde Tabbi Memorial University for dinner.

The Cultural Attaché had only asked Dr Trotter one question: 'Any newspapers?'

Dr Trotter said that he hadn't any. 'Just didn't think,' he added.

'Typical!' the Cultural Attaché replied.

Dr Trotter nodded to the united nations of lecturers seated around the table in the guest house dining room. One or two lecturers nodded back, but there was silence in the hot room except for the buzzing of flies and loud voices emanating from what Dr Trotter assumed must be the kitchen. Dr Trotter sat down and looked at the blank faces opposite. He desperately tried to think of something to say, but could only think, 'Set amidst the rolling countryside on the fringes of Working-ton . . .' and he did not think that such an utterance would be suitable.

The kitchen door opened and two tall waiters, trying to keep straight faces, burst into the room and banged steaming bowls of yams on to the table. They then retreated to the kitchen, slamming the door irreverently.

'What, no meat?' asked a very tired-looking blonde at the head of the table.

'Looks like it,' said her companion.

Silence returned as everyone dug into the bowls morosely.

'Excuse me,' said Dr Trotter, 'might I have the salt, please?'

His companion passed him the salt and asked, 'You new?'

Dr Trotter brightened. 'Well, yes. But I'm just passing through.'

'Lucky you! Where are you going?'

'I'm travelling round the country. Recruitment drive.'

The man nodded.

'God help you!' said the woman at the end of the table.

'Hope so!' breezed back Dr Trotter.

The next morning, Dr Trotter returned to the airport with the Cultural Attaché.

'Bring me back a newspaper or something from wherever you're going, will you?'

'Yes, I will.'

Dr Trotter put his bag on the scales. Then he took out his ticket. When he looked back his – or rather Gwen's – suitcase, had gone.

'The flight is full,' said the man.

'He says the flight is full!' exclaimed Dr Trotter, turning back towards the Cultural Attaché, who, like the suitcase, had also disappeared.

He turned back to the man. 'But it says "O.K." on it!'

'Did you reconfirm?' asked the man.

'Well, no I didn't. Actually.'

'But you want to go to Ofingi today?'

'That is what I'd planned. Yes.'

'Give me fifty jumpas.'

Dr Trotter reached into his wallet and handed over fifty jumpas, wondering what the Chancellor of Goldsworthy College of Advanced Business Studies would make of the extra expenditure.

The man gave him a boarding pass.

Dr Trotter walked towards the Departure Lounge. He passed

through an open area. There was some wire on one side and behind the wire stood a man in green coveralls and beside the man sat Dr Trotter's wife's suitcase.

'Do you want this suitcase to go on the flight to Ofingi?' asked the man in green coveralls, furtively.

'Yes, please,' said Dr Trotter. He felt like saying that he would not have checked his luggage if he hadn't wanted it to proceed to Ofingi – but didn't think the merry traditional wit of the pedagogue was exactly what the situation called for.

'Give me one hundred jumpas and it will,' said the man.

Dr Trotter thought for a moment, but then he thought of all the educational material and applications forms in the bag. He gave the man a disapproving frown as he handed him the hundred jumpas.

The man took the money without thanking Dr Trotter, and slouched away with his suitcase.

'This is the unacceptable face of capitalism,' Dr Trotter told the wire. The wire twanged and jangled in the wind blowing across the runway.

An Englishman wearing a white bandage around his head greeted Dr Trotter at Ofingi Airport.

'Dr Trotter?' he asked.

'Oh, yes!' exclaimed Dr Trotter, pleased to see a friendly face.

The Englishman in the white bandage made for the door and Dr Trotter followed him feeling as light as air. Why, even his heavy suitcase felt lighter.

In the Landrover the Englishman said, 'It's all chaos, I'm afraid. We had an armed robbery last night.'

'An armed robbery? Goodness, I *am* sorry!' said Dr Trotter sympathetically.

'They went through the College floor by floor.'

'Did they? Tut-tut.'

'Turned off the electricity before they started.'

'My!'

'Most of the students are in the hospital and the faculty's taking refuge at the British Council. That's where we're heading.'

Dr Trotter was startled. 'But what about my talk?'

'What about it?' asked the Englishman.

'I'm sorry,' said Dr Trotter, 'that was rather insensitive of me.'

'It was, rather,' said the bandaged Englishman.

'Not another one,' sighed Charlotte Plunkett, the famous anthropologist and wife of the British Council representative in Ofingi.

''Fraid so,' said the bandaged Englishman.

'Well put him over there, next to the hubble-bubble pipe,' said Charlotte. Then she turned back to comforting a weeping young man with a bandage around his head and, Dr Trotter noted, wearing exactly the same kind of glasses he, Dr Trotter, was wearing. That was comforting in a way.

Dr Trotter sat down. All around him were English people with bandages on their heads.

'I'm Dr Trotter from the Goldsworthy College of Advanced Business Studies,' said Dr Trotter to a man sprawled over two camel bags to the right of the hubble-bubble pipe.

'Recruitment?' asked the man, feeling the bandage on his neck.

'Yes. At least I hope so,' said Dr Trotter.

'The name's Rafferty,' said the man. 'I arrived yesterday. London School of Economics.'

'I see. I arrived a bit late then,' said Dr Trotter.

'Any earlier and you'd have a bandage round your head,' said Rafferty, then he said 'Ouch!'

'What's the matter?'

'Machete wounds playing up again. Don't take any notice of me. Is this your last stop?'

'No, my first. Well, my second, if you count Tabbitown.'

'You're going round anti-clockwise, then?'

'Yes, I suppose I am, though I must admit that I hadn't looked at it in those terms,' replied Dr Trotter.

'I did it clockwise.'

'Oh, so you've probably swept up all the best students, have you?' smiled Dr Trotter, though deep inside his heart was breaking.

Rafferty groaned then said, 'You'll find out!'

''Spect so!' said Dr Trotter.

A week later, Dr Trotter was once again asking for the salt for his plate of yams in the guest house dining room of Isolde Tabbi Memorial University. He had arrived at the airport and remembered when he saw the Cultural Attaché that he had forgotten to remember to buy him his newspaper. The Cultural Attaché had treated him even more peremptorily than previously, making him sit in the back of the Landrover next to a half-inflated lilo, cradling the wreckage of Gwen's Antler suitcase on his knee.

When asked by the worn blonde woman how things had gone, he gave a sigh which reminded him of Rafferty's moan.

'The plane couldn't land at Petula City because the insurgents had taken over the control tower at the airport and were broadcasting revolutionary Reggae songs instead of instructions for landing; in Tiwi someone had bombed the TabbiCola bottling plant and a twenty-four hour curfew was in force. I had had to pay so much departure tax at the airports that I could not afford to go on to Mumby.'

'So here you are.'

'Yes, here I am. I don't know what the chancellor will say, I really don't. We are threatened with closure, you see.'

The woman nodded.

'You might be able to get a job here,' she said.

'Oh, no thank you,' replied Dr Trotter. 'I think I would prefer to take early retirement. I'm the age.'

'I wish I were,' said the woman.

In order to leave Porsellana, Dr Trotter had had to make a gift of his Taiwanese Leatherette briefcase to the Porsellair official because he was completely bereft of funds. He had no confidence that he would ever see his wife's Antler suitcase again because he had had to shrug when the man on the other side of the wire had asked for one hundred jumpas. Then, the man at the final security check had taken him behind a curtain and made him remove his jacket, saying that only if he were allowed to keep it as a present 'to souvenir you by' would Dr Trotter be allowed through on to his flight. Dr Trotter had nodded and sighed.

When the seat-belt sign was turned off, the world-famous, bare-breasted cabin crew of Porsellair offered coconut shells of palm beer, and Dr Trotter, sitting relaxed in shirt sleeves, drank three.

After dinner, when the drum started to beat ominously from the galley and the Bursar appeared in his black loin cloth, playing the Ongu drum and readying the economy cabin for its post-prandial Sky Spirits Dance, Dr Trotter, perhaps because of the palm beer and the bottle of Tabbi Sauvignon '87, felt his feet tapping to the rhythm.

It took only the outstretched hand of welcome from a world-famous bare-breasted flight attendant to get Dr Trotter to his feet. His brochures and application forms for the Goldsworthy College of Advanced Business Studies slipped from his lap and turned the floor festive as Dr Trotter got up and danced in the confined space at the front of Economy. And as he danced, he consigned worry and regret and explanation and early-retirement to the morrow, and let the justly world-famous Ongu drum, beating to a pulp the drone of the twentieth century jet, tell him what life is, after all, all about.

Even the Mice Know

The old woman entered the elevator on the twenty-ninth floor just as Ed Welch had started to think he was going to be alone the whole way down. She entered slowly, leaning on a walking frame. Ed Welch held the Door Open button for her.

Once inside, she spoke through her smile across the elevator as it plummeted to earth.

'Only five more days,' she said.

Her smile cleared her face of age as a high wind will a street of autumn leaves. Ed Welch watched the smile, saw the old lady as she might have been half a century ago, at once compared the sight of her, unfavourably, with his own soul – but completely missed what she had said.

For Ed Welch had been feeling even more disturbed since getting into the elevator; wondering if the elevator was, in fact, still in control and suspended from the metal rope which yo-yoed it up and down the building a thousand times a day – or whether, just for him on this day, a day when by rights it should not matter, the elevator had decided to part company from its helpmate, the wire. When the old woman spoke he had been wondering what happened to bodies after they had undergone the fall from twenty-nine floors to the ground. If he jumped high in the air round about the third floor, would he come out unscathed?

'Oh yes?' he replied.

The old lady dropped her smile and became old again. Ed Welch attempted to smile at her, but it did no good. No, he thought. Sure as eggs are eggs he'd be scrambled by the impact just like everybody else. He shivered.

'Yes, only five more days.'

Of course! Of course he knew exactly what the old woman was referring to. It was so obvious. Every street in San Francisco proclaimed it: lights on all the buildings; the piles of pointless poinsettias everywhere; the video store outside the apartment building showing a film in its window, hour after hour, of a log fire burning, with stockings hung. (How would Santa make his way through that inferno?) Yes, all things proclaimed it. But Ed Welch, still apprehensive about the lift, despairing, feeling hatred gobbling up the man he had been a mere week before, pressed his thick-lensed spectacles against the bridge of his nose and decided to be opaque with the old woman. He smiled and said, 'Really?' noting that the lift had come to the sixth floor.

It would soon be time to jump for it if any time was the time to jump. But he couldn't tell the old woman to jump. He decided not to jump. He would let whatever would happen happen. He would be dying in good company.

She was looking at him quizzically, both her hands resting on the walking frame. She was small and slightly stooped, with a face now like an abrupt, efficient housekeeper hedgehog in a children's story.

The elevator came harmlessly to rest at the first floor as it always had and he hoped for the old woman's sake if not his own, please God, always would. The doors opened. Ed Welch walked out of the elevator with her, measuring his pace, guarding her like some Victorian angel minding a child across a river. She gazed up at him once or twice, a child wondering what this strange apparition was up to.

At last they reached the centre of the lobby of the apartment building. There, she turned to – or rather on – him and said, 'Yes. Five more days. Five more!' as if she were addressing somebody very deaf or very dense.

'Sorry?' he asked, enjoying the game he was playing.

The old woman sighed and shook her head slowly towards

the walking frame. 'You mean you don't know? You really don't know?' she asked him.

'Know what?' he asked, thinking of Scrooge and the empty apartment he had left behind on the forty-seventh floor, his depression suddenly back – where had it gone while he had been helping the old lady? – and pounding like a migraine.

She continued on across the lobby and fixed him with a hard stare. 'I have to check my mail box. Goodbye.'

'I'd offer to check it for you but I know you want the exercise,' he said.

'Well, I'm glad you know something,' replied the old woman, wounding him strangely, making him lift his hand to protest, to protect himself. But then he deflected his arm and made his hand stroke his unshaven chin instead.

He left her there. Albert the doorman opened the door for him and wished him the compliments of the season. Ed Welch smiled and thought he ought to remember to tip the man before he left.

Outside it would soon be getting dark. The city had been swathed in low cloud all day but now, out towards the Golden Gate bridge, he saw that the sun was about to put in a brief appearance on the horizon. Just above it the bank of cloud ended and a thin strip of blue promised a fine day on the morrow. Out in the Pacific everything would be bright and golden. He thought of his ticket. Tomorrow morning he would be going west – though he did not want to; could hardly bear to.

'Now, what do I have to do?' he asked himself.

He knew there was a lot to be done. He fumbled about in the untidy drawers of his brain marked 'wants, needs, whims', extracted from them a list of what to do, get and enquire about, trying to place everything in some sort of order of priority.

He passed the Bon Appetit supermarket and thought of the old woman. Had she arrived at her mailbox yet? She would probably be bound for the supermarket but it would take her an age. He wondered if he should have offered to do her shopping for her but was sure that the tough old bird would have taken such an offer amiss.

Anyway, he wished her well. She was the first human being he had spoken to since it had happened.

Then he saw himself on his plane heading out and thinking of her as the plane nosed towards Singapore. He knew he would think of her then. Better to think of a sweet old woman than of . . .

He walked up Sacramento Street, passing young business-people. He did not know why, but they seemed dangerous, somehow threatening, to him in their sharp suits. They had hardly a glance for him. He had had his day and looked it.

'Spare a quarter for a cup of coffee, sir.'

Ed Welch was on top of the beggar before he saw him. He fumbled in his pockets, saying, 'Er . . . well . . .' as he did so, firmly focusing his gaze on the sidewalk at his feet. Almost in a panic he searched for change, finally finding some in the pocket which held his revolver. He took some out and tossed it into the man's paper cup. Then he walked on hastily.

As he did so, he heard, 'Compliments of the season to you, sir! My heartfelt thanks, sir!' enunciated by a voice that would have done justice to a reading of Walt Whitman in a large auditorium.

He half turned and nodded. But if the beggar noticed he did not say anything else.

Ed Welch thought how embarrassing it was to show small acts of generosity. The money parted with was by a long way the least of it. It hardly figured at all in fact. No, rather, the generosity, the virtue of giving to someone in need in a public place, was to scramble for the coins while under the gaze of a maybe-critical populace; then, having found the coins, to make the quick dart to the recipient while still under public scrutiny. Did those passers-by think him silly, soft, or, worst of all, a Holy Joe? Then, of course, did the recipient think he had been generous enough? And what about God?

He remembered one single, uncluttered act of charity while working in Madras years before. At his filling station, every Monday, a woman in a tattered, oily sari had filled up his car. Every Monday he said 'Fill her up!' and every week she had done so and then charged him five rupees more than she should have done. Yet every week he donated those five rupees to the woman, knowing as he did so that she probably thought him a fool. He never tipped the woman. Indeed he was always rather brusque with her and each time he drove away from the filling station he felt as if he had been cheated. The act did not make him feel good – and that had to be good.

He found that he had walked his way too far up Sacramento. He stopped, trying to recall what he was seeking. Was it a want, a need, or a whim? He could not remember but reasoned that if he could not remember it was, in all probability, a whim. He turned on his heel and walked back down the street, distracted now by the sight of the chock-full Bay Bridge hopping over the East Bay to Oakland. Gertrude Stein, he recalled, had said that the trouble with Oakland was that there was no 'there' there – whatever that meant.

'Spare a quarter for a cup of coffee, sir!'

'You've already done me,' Ed Welch replied, but not loud enough for anyone but himself to hear. Then he repeated the phrase to the fog above him that furled and foamed and blocked the Ears of the God he now addressed. He smiled wryly.

He had walked on past the man but suddenly stopped, and searched his pockets again. He retraced his steps and gave the man all the change he was able to find. He gazed at the paper cup doggedly.

'Thank you again, sir. Good luck to you! May the New Year bring joy to you and your family.'

'I haven't got a family, I'm afraid, but thank you for your compliments. I wish you all the best too.'

The beggar did not say anything further and Ed turned away and continued down Sacramento and then turned on to Sansome Street, trying to think of his important wants and needs.

He arrived at Market Street but was still unable to remember a single thing he had to do. He shrugged inwardly and decided that that must mean that there really was nothing further to be done. Then he nodded at the truth of that. He had emptied everything out. All traces of his dead family had been packed up and collected by Goodwill. What did he need on his journey? You could buy paper handkerchiefs in Singapore, couldn't you? Probably some enterprising vendor would be selling them outside the mortuary. What did he need – apart from a wife and two grown daughters whom he had been about to 'get off his hands'? Well, they were off his hands now, weren't they? Were they? He found that he had brought his fingers up to his face and was sniffing them.

It would be hard getting on to the plane. He would, no doubt, feel terrible when confronted with the plastic wall covering of the cabin and the seats that must be the same kind of seat his wife and daughters had sat in, been strapped into and then clung to and wept against and then screamed and despaired in. Had they panicked? Had they rushed around the cabin in the minutes between the emergency and the crash? Or had they sat holding hands across the three seats bidding farewell and watching the clouds outside – tears streaming – as the plane plummeted? Had they thought of him?

On second thoughts, he decided, he did need something. He went into a drug-store and bought a packet of double-sided razor blades. He found his face would not function to ask the salesgirl the price. His mouth was dry, as if stuffed full of powdered bone.

Then, back on Market Street, he watched the rush-hour traffic for a minute, standing stock still and panting like a dog.

'Is everything all right, sir?' a young woman asked him.

He nodded to the woman. 'Yes. Thank you. You see . . . it's just . . . I must go home.' And he fled back along Battery Street towards the apartment building.

He had recovered himself by the time he passed Bon Appetit; had even managed to remember all the things he had forgotten to do, though he did not care that he had forgotten.

And he was not in the least surprised when he saw the old woman struggling back from the supermarket, crammed bags hanging from the walking frame.

'Remember me?' he asked her.

'A guy with total amnesia is not that easy to forget,' replied the old woman. She stopped for a rest.

'It's taken you a while to do your marketing,' he said.

'I've got time.'

'Now you must let me help you carry your parcels. They must be slowing you down.'

He reached over to take one of the bags but she slapped his hand.

'No!' she almost shouted, and startled him.

'But surely . . .'

'Do you know yet?'

'Know what?'

'What everybody knows.'

He was back in the game begun in the lift. 'No. What?'

'You must know! Why even the mice know!'

She looked concerned, almost on the verge of tears. He decided that the game had gone far enough. She really did think that he didn't know. He *did* know. The trouble was that he did not feel.

'Yes, Christmas is coming,' he said flatly.

'Right. You can carry my things for me now, though I warn you, you're in for a slow walk home.'

He took the two heavy bags from the walking frame and walked beside her back towards the apartment building. He bent towards her like a willow bends over a stream and listened to her speaking. And as he listened the weight of the last week – of all of his fifty-five years – lifted itself off him, lightened him, as his lifting of the bags had lightened the walking frame. His loneliness and despair and wild plans for vengeance dissolved as he listened and took tiny baby-steps beside the old woman.

'I must leave you now,' she told him as the lift opened at her floor.

He nodded, held the Door Open button for her and she slowly walked out of his life. The lift door drew shut behind her.

Back in his empty apartment he took the revolver from his pocket, wrapped it in several plastic bags and dropped it down the refuse shute. Then he sent the razor blades the same way and walked out on to his balcony.

The clock on the Ferry Building, far below him to his left, struck six and then the bells launched into a Christmas carol to which he could not put a name.

'I will go to Singapore and identify the bodies. Then I shall return and help the old woman with her shopping.'

He laughed at the foolishness of the idea but consoled himself that that idea was less foolish than others he had had in the past week.

Then, quite suddenly, completely taken by surprise as he leaned against the guard-rail gazing down and out over the Ferry Building and the Bay Bridge and the dark water and the lights of Oakland, he was weeping. The bells finished the carol and he could hear himself bawling like an infant, feel the snot pouring out of his nose, as tears flooded from his eyes and down his face; plummeting earthward – past all the balconies below his – and on to the sidewalk where old women struggle and beggars ask for aid and where, perhaps, when everyone is tucked up in their beds, the mice come out and tell one another what they know.

On the Left Side

Anyone who visits St Finbar's during Sunday mass will be fascinated by the queer seating arrangements. The right side of the church is filled to bursting while only ten people – myself and nine other sinners – sit on the left.

It's a huge church, St Finbar's, built during the Troubles by rebellious Canon O'Rourke to cock a snook at the Church of Ireland pile nearby. And in those early days it was filled to bursting every Sunday. But the population of Conn, County Mayo, has decreased since – I often think we Irish are just bred for export – and the pews are only half filled most weeks. In the sixties a rich farmer left the church some money in his will on condition that it was spent on providing some heat for the church, a draughty place even in summer and enough to turn the Pope protestant in winter. Father O'Rourke, a great-nephew of the church's builder, reluctantly shelled out on enough electric wall-heaters to heat half the church. The right half. The left was left as it had been and was used not at all, except by the odd mad tourist. The whole congregation made a bee-line for the right side – until, that is, Sister Philomena O'Halloran sent us her Christmas present.

We in Conn have always prided ourselves on our missionary activity. Rows of competing missionary boxes have lined the counter at Hephernan's grocers ever since I was a girl. Old man Hephernan would dish out the change in tiny denominations and would take a very dim view of anyone who left his shop without making the missionary boxes clink. Failure to contribute had been known to cut the miser's credit to the bone. At school we saved black babies by the gross, cured lepers past computation. Most of us had never been further than Castlebar but our influence – or so we were taught – spread itself far and wide across the heathen world.

So we were all very excited when Father O'Rourke announced that the other half of the farmer's money was to be spent on a very special charity. Conn was to send one of its daughters to Burundi to set up and run a medical mission. The town was agog, wondering who would be chosen. There were a lot to choose from. Conn produced nuns and nurses and combinations of the two as other towns produce, say, tweed or tea cosies. At last news reached us that Philomena O'Halloran of the Poor Sisters of St Thaddeus had been picked.

Philomena O'Halloran, a small nun with twinkling blue eyes and the O'Hallorans' prominent chin, was given a special mass and breakfast before being seen off on the Dublin train. The missionary boxes disappeared overnight from pub, shop and church door to be replaced by one, the Sister Philomena fund. And Mr Hephernan began saying as he handed people their change, 'Here's your Philomena money.'

To his credit he never stopped saying it, though a few years later a supermarket opened on the outskirts of the town, robbing him of much custom. Ireland joined the Common Market and poor farmers discarded their donkeys and bought Austin eleven hundreds, left thatched cottages to rot and built white bungalows. Irish towns began to be twinned with unpronounceable places on the Continent whose people came to visit us and bought the discarded cottages of the newly rich farmers. Conn, however, was twinned with Obtu, Burundi, where Sister Philomena continued to fight the good fight out of sight, but never quite out of mind.

We heard news of our African apostolate seated on the right side of St Finbar's each Sunday. Father O'Rourke read us letters from Philomena O'Halloran and held special collections more often than some thought was called for, saying that he wanted to hear the rustle of notes rather than the jingling of change. A noticeboard at the back of the church showed us pictures of what was being wrought in the African forests. We saw row upon row of smiling African children, Sister Philomena injecting black arms, comforting the old and the lame. She had discarded her navy-blue habit for a blouse and a pair of shorts – something which raised the eyebrows of a number of conservatives – but there was no denying that much was being achieved.

Conn had been supporting the Sister Philomena mission for over two decades when Sister Philomena wrote that she was going to send us a Christmas present in the form of a young man from the mission. The young man's father, she said, would pay the fare but it would be appreciated if accommodation could be offered. I offered but so did everybody else and in the end the Widow Hephernan was chosen. The Widow Hephernan lived alone (Grocer Hephernan having passed on to his reward in 1981) in a large house. To provide hospitality to a real live African was seen as the pinnacle of achievement. And this African had been brought up by our own special saint.

A group of Conn notables was waiting on the station for the arrival of the Dublin train. I watched from a distance, eating a Crunchie by the ticket window and making eyes at Declan Lyons the station master, who's far too nice to be a bachelor. The train arrived a few minutes early for a change. I should have known then that something was up. A full minute passed, during which time I finished my Crunchie and wondered whether I should go off and spread the news that the African had failed to arrive. But had I done that I would have opened myself to castigation from the pulpit on the Sunday following for, just as my legs ached to hoof off to O'Flaherty's, a small figure appeared at the far end of the platform, holding a brown suitcase. He looked up the platform towards the group and then started walking towards it.

As the young man approached I saw Father O'Rourke's jaw drop, quickly followed by those of the rest of the group. I could not at first see what had caused their surprise but when the lad came closer I dropped my Crunchie wrapper and had not Declan Lyons drawn attention to my lapse I do not think I would have noticed.

The sight of the young African was a shock. He was lighter than most Africans, a beautiful creamed-coffee colour. It was his face, though, which caused the jaws of Conn to drop and in the days that followed got them wagging. For the African had cornflower blue eyes and the O'Halloran chin.

'Hello,' he said. 'My name's Friday Mkete. I have come to spend Christmas with my benefactors.'

'What sort of name is Friday for a Christian?' asked Father O'Rourke looking suspicious.

Now I, being a simple sort of girl, who has read her Tarzan books to Leaving Certificate level, would have thought the answer to that was obviously that Friday was called Friday because he had been born on a Friday. Friday, however, surprised us.

'My father is called Thursday.'

That appealed to me greatly. What everybody with the least acquaintance with the O'Halloran physiognomy – just about everyone with eyes – wanted to know was what had Thursday done to Sister Philomena? It seemed as clear as the chin on your face that it was something which had dawned as Friday. And, if our presentiments were right, what on earth had got into Philomena to let her sin find her out after all those years?

The thing was that nobody had the courage to ask the question. In the days before Christmas, had anyone plucked up the required puff to climb Ben Brandon – the mountain that broods over Conn – and look back down at the town, he

would have seen written above it as if in sky-writing, IS
PHILOMENA O'HALLORAN YOUR MOTHER? Nobody did, of
course. I remember when Friday's picture appeared on the
front of the Conn Advertiser seeing the Widow Hephernan
poring over the picture and comparing the likeness to that of
Sister Philomena on the front of the mission box. When the
Widow Hephernan saw me seeing her she stood up straight
and asked me what she could do for me in a way that
betokened that if she had her way nothing further could or
would be done for me, seeing as I was a fallen woman. Still,
I'm used to such looks. I've been fallen long enough – down
so long it seems like up to me, as the unwilling emigrants that
share Friday's blood might say.

In the event, though, the question did not need to be asked
because Friday told us without the least prompting. He had
been taken on a pilgrimage down to O'Flaherty's bar by some
buckoes who had been feeling that it must be miserable for a
poor African to be at the Widow Hephernan's, forced to eat
pilchard sandwiches with the crust cut off, drink gallons of
tea and kneel down to the rosary as soon as Telefís Éireann
was off the air. The buckoes took no notice of Widow
Hephernan's looks, even though it would probably send their
credit rating at Hephernan's grocers to the devil. Friday
downed a pint of Guinness faster than a monsignor or a
bookie on his way back from Kildare, remarking that it was
not as strong as African beer. Then he said, as bold as brass,
that his mum made the best hooch south of the Tanzam
railroad – whatever that is when it's at home.

'Tell us about your mum, Friday.'

And Friday did.

This happened on the night before Christmas Eve, so the
news of Sister Philomena's disgrace had a full day to spread
around Conn before Christmas Mass.

The right side of the church was packed out when Friday
came in alone. The Widow Hephernan had obviously decided

that the shame was too great for her to put in an appearance. He walked down the aisle with every eye in the place on him. He did not seem at all concerned, but took his seat in the very front row on the left.

Mass began and I swear that nobody in the church was paying the least attention to the goings-on at the altar. All eyes were glued to the single brown man on the left side of the church. When the time came for the sermon, Father O'Rourke mounted the steps of the pulpit with a face of thunder and launched into a sermon about the Last Judgement – one we would expect to hear at the start of Lent rather than on the day of our Saviour's birth. He talked of the good on the right of God and the wicked on the left. He talked of whited sepulchres and sins against holy purity and the torment meted out to hypocrites.

I sat there going hot and cold with a mixture of anger, embarrassment and fear. It was as clear as the nose on your face that Father O'Rourke was addressing Philomena O'Halloran sitting there in front of him in the form of Friday Mkete. I had received similar treatment when I told Father O'Rourke about my baby – though mercifully in the little cubby hole of confession. But the public humiliation being meted out to this innocent lad made me angry in a way I had never been angry before. I wanted to stand up and protest. Then I thought I should walk out and never darken the doors of St Finbar's again. But I sat. Father O'Rourke kept on and on about the sheep on the right and the goats on the left and suddenly a strange thing happened. Simultaneously a few of the congregation stood up, pushed their way to the centre aisle, genuflected and went and sat on Friday's side of the church. It took me a while to realise what was happening but when I did I went and joined them. Friday had not even looked round. I am not sure to this day whether he was aware of what was happening.

That might have been enough but it didn't end there.

Father O'Rourke – truly a man with all the finesse of a
Mullingar heifer – finished his hellfire sermon, making no
mention of Christmas or the special collection for Burundi,
and returned to the altar. Then, during the offertory I saw
Miss Dwyer, who is Father O'Rourke's housekeeper and in
charge of St Finbar's crib, leave her place on the right and
disappear into the sacristy. She emerged a minute later with a
statue of one of the three kings – the black one – and trundled
it across the front of the church, though it was almost as big
as herself and must have weighed like a sack of spuds.
Behind the curtain covering the crib until after Mass she
went, every eye in the place, including Father O'Rourke's, on
her. There were some sounds of scraping and back she came
and sat herself down next to me – slipping me a merry wink –
in good time for the consecration.

Father O'Rourke elevated the Host, his hands shaking
visibly, and we all – on right and left – bowed our heads as
we had been taught. I said a prayer for Philomena O'Halloran
in the middle of her twentieth Christmas away from home
but with her felix culpa, her greatest achievement, kneeling in
front of us.

After mass Father O'Rourke asked Miss Dwyer why she
had placed one of the three kings in the crib when they are
not supposed to arrive until the Epiphany.

'Sure didn't this one arrive early?' she replied.

Well, Friday Mkete returned to Africa many Guinnesses
later. Miss Dwyer still keeps house for Father O'Rourke,
though he no longer has special collections for the Philomena
mission. The Widow Hephernan has removed her box from
the counter of her shop. Those of us who sat on the left side
of the church that Christmas Eve still do, and we do our best
to collect money among the sinners and publicans of County
Mayo. What we are able to send to Philomena is not as much
as before but she seems to be managing. Still, it's a bit cold
over here on the left of the church, away from the heat and

the good sheep. We just wrap up warm and try to keep cheerful.

And usually we do, thank God.

Worried About Dolores

Many had been to the saint before her that day. Many came every day to the statue of the young nun of Lisieux who had promised after her death to drop miracles on the earth like roses. The statue stood behind two dozen burning candles, a smiling girl in a Carmelite habit, holding a crucifix to her breast, while with the other hand she dropped the promised roses down her body, past her rosary and on to the earth beneath her feet.

Dolores put fifty cents in the collection box, took a candle from the tray and lit it, holding the wick next to one already-burning plea. Then she fixed the candle into the bottom-most space on the candle-holder, hoping that her humility would endear her to the saint, make her pay more attention to her than to the more confident candles burning a jot nearer heaven. She knelt down on the prie-dieu, looking up, through the soft candle-light, to the kindly wimpled face of the statue.

'It's me, dear St Thérèse. It's Dolores. I am sorry to bother you. I can see that you are busy. But every time I come you are busy, so I suppose one time is no worse than another. I am not even sure that you are the saint I should be approaching. It is habit, I guess. When I was younger, when I was innocent, it seemed fitting to come to you for help because you were young and innocent when you died. You, like me, had never strayed far from your village. Dying at twenty-four with all those innocent sisters around you, I always thought you would understand the problems of a young village girl like me. Ah, but St Thérèse, I did not know then what was going to become of me. I could not see the miles I should have to travel, the houses of strangers, the insinuating touches of men who held my passport and the future of my family in their evil hands. St Thérèse, I could tell you stories! The good die young, they say. I think I have many years ahead of me.

'I sometimes look in my Dictionary of the Saints, trying to find one who had sinned as I have sinned, who would not be shocked by what I have to say. There were, of course, many and I do pray to them in the quiet of my room. But here in St Patrick's I must take what is on offer. Many go to St Joseph over there. But he is a man, although a most exceptional man. He took Mary back and believed that she was a virgin. No man that I have ever known would believe that. He would think that what the angel had told him about Mary and the Holy Ghost was a lie. He would get up and take off his belt to beat her, or maybe use it to sharpen his knife upon. No, pretend I didn't say that! What do you know about such things?

'I hate to think that all the requests of poor sinners here below may be stopping you from enjoying heaven. But perhaps it is possible for you to continue in rapture in God's sight while still paying attention to our needs. Even here on earth some people can do many things at the same time. Mrs Duke's children can listen to their Walkmen, talk to one another and yet can still kill the soldiers on the television with their computer guns. I don't know how they can do all these things at one and the same time. If I am ironing in the next room and hear the bang of their toy guns and the cries of the dying cartoon soldiers, I find that I am losing concentration and will forget to iron a cuff. Mrs Duke doesn't seem to worry about distractions either. She can talk to a friend on the telephone and switch channels on her television set and massage cream into her face and make sure her cup of coffee warming in the microwave doesn't boil over. All these things she can do. I guess that is why they are all so rich in New York. They can do things in half the time. A simple Filipina like me can do only one thing.

'I'm sorry, St Thérèse, I am such a gossip. I only meant to say that if people down below can do many things at the same time then you in heaven may be able to listen to our prayers and requests and problems while at the same time enjoying everything heaven has to offer. Yes, I am sure you can do that. I mean, heaven would not be heaven if you were denied it every time you had to listen to a request. Anyway, thank you for your attention. I am an unworthy sinner. I know that I do not merit any of the roses you have promised to send down to the world.

'Yes. I, Dolores, am a wicked girl. I keep thinking that maybe I am wicked because I am poor. But that is no excuse, is it? I sometimes look into my mirror and wonder why men see me as a girl who is prepared to be wicked. I never wear dresses cut more than half a little finger below the neck. I refused several of the dresses that Mrs Duke offered me for that reason. Mrs Duke wears very revealing dreses, but she is a good woman and no men ever take advantage of her. But it seems that ever since I left my village men have seen me as the kind of girl who is available.

'I thought when I came to the Duke household that things would be different. Mr Duke is a doctor as I am sure you know. He has beautiful white hair and was interested in everything I told him about my life. When I said how I had been treated when I was sent to Arabia I thought he was going to cry. He kept saying, "O my gosh, O my gosh!" And I did not tell him everything. I only told him how one of the sons had forced me to be impure. But there was much more to say. I could have told him about the agent's man in Manila. The agent laughed when I said that I was an honest girl and a teacher of English in my village. He knew I was poor. He knew that my whole family needed me to get a job abroad in order to support them. He knew he had the power. I wanted to say no. I have always wanted to say no, but if I had said no I would have lost the jobs, and my family would have lost the food from their mouths. So I said yes.

'If Sebastian knew he would be angry. I know he would not

marry me. He might take a knife to me and end my life. But what can I do? I have to stay away from my country. I have to send money home. And I am just one of millions.

'St Thérèse, you must have heard this story so many times before. Perhaps it makes you yawn. No, I'm sorry, I did not mean that. I know that you are interested in all our problems. The sisters always used to tell me that a prayer did not need to be full of words. And here I am babbling like I babble when I meet another Filipina maid on my night off. Of course we don't talk like I'm talking now – well, not all the time. We also talk about Green Cards and going home and what is happening there and how we can send our money or the things that relatives are always writing to us and asking us to send them. That is one of the biggest problems, St Thérèse. People think that because I am in rich New York I have got plenty of money to send them all the things they do not have. I try to. I send pens and books and little gadgets, but Grandmother wrote me asking for a dehumidifier. I did not even know what a dehumidifier was, but Grandma knew because there is a consumer programme on Manila television called *Whatever Next?* and they showed Grandma a machine that takes the water out of the air and Grandma has been obsessed with the idea of it ever since. She keeps telling Mama that she would sell her soul to the devil for a dehumidifier because a dehumidifier would take water out of the air and make her breathing easier. I do not judge Grandma harshly, dear St Thérèse. She has worked so hard all her life and has had little chance to buy comforts. Now that she has a relative in America it is natural that she should do her best to receive favours. For Grandma I am perhaps as you are to me, an invisible benefactor. But already I send them every dollar that remains from my wages. How can I send money for a dehumidifier? Perhaps Dolores knows how you feel, St Thérèse. I too feel besieged sometimes.

'You must be so busy and yet here I am going on and on. I saw a picture in a Philipino newspaper last week of President Aquino praying to you in a Manila church. Poor President Aquino! I can

only imagine what a long list she presented to you for your
attention. What a headache! She must not only pray for the
repose of the soul of her dead husband but for all of the
millions of Filipinos she is in charge of. Listen to her, dear
saint. Listen to her first. I am only one.

'But I do have a problem – I mean apart from the *real*
problem. All our prayers are answered. Did not Jesus say that?
So what did you do when Ferdinand and Imelda Marcos
prayed to you? They had everything on earth that anybody
could possibly want, a million times more. But what they did
not have was the love of the people. I just do not understand,
St Thérèse, how a leader would not care about what the people
thought of them. Would our love not bring them more
satisfaction than all the jewels and shoes and real estate in the
world? Imagine what we would have done for them when they
died, had they really loved us and worked only for us! We
would have set up shrines to them, had masses said, named
streets after them, cherished their memory as blessed. But I
have seen what they did with the money they stole. Ferdinand
and Imelda loved it more than all of the millions of poor
Filipinos. How can this be? Explain it to me. I want to
understand. I say a prayer for Imelda. I ask you to teach her
the right way.

'I think I am babbling so much because I am really afraid to
tell you what I need. Let me tell you what has happened. Last
week Mrs Duke went out with the children. They were going
to spend the day with friends in Connecticut. Dr Duke came in
and started talking to me about my life in the Philippines. I told
him how poor we are, how everyone is dependent on me. I
told him about Grandma and her aches and pains. I also
described Smoky Mountain, where Sebastian searches with a
stick through all the rubbish of Manila and takes as prizes the
things that I throw down the Duke's refuse-chute twice a day –
tears in my eyes at the thought that the objects here are
without value, while on Smoky Mountain the uncovering of a

can would make Sebastian's heart beat faster. Dr Duke said
that my story made him ashamed to have all that he had, but I
told him that everything in the world is as God intended and
that anyway he had been very kind to me. Then, St Thérèse,
he walked over to me where I was sitting ironing, and stroked
my hair. I was not anxious. Actually I looked at his gold Rolex
and did a sum about what it would buy for me back in Manila.
It made me giddy. It would, of course, buy everything I dream
of. I do not think it means much to him. He throws it on the
bedside table each night as I throw cans down the refuse-
chute. Perhaps with less care than that. Anyway I was not
scared when he stroked me because it felt like a father
comforting me. But then he pinched my cheek, leaned down
and kissed me. "Please, Mr Duke," I said. "I am a good girl."

'"You forget," he replied. "I've heard your story."'

'Now, St Thérèse, this is the part that I know you are going
to hate to hear, you whose Holy Purity was a byword throughout France. But if I do not tell you I cannot tell anyone. I have
been used before. In Arabia the father and his brothers, even
the eldest son, thought that because they were rich all they had
to do was click their fingers and I would do it with them. I
resisted then but they knew their way through my defences,
through every defence of workers from poor countries. "We
will report you to the Ministry of Alien Labour for insub-
ordination and theft." They had the power. I had visited
Filipina maids in stinking prisons, their only crime refusing to
give the men what they wanted. But these men were like
children in their sex. They were so excited and afraid that it
was over before it had begun. A few stabs, a moan and
stickiness. I would watch them, St Thérèse, watch them
completely detached, and think, "So this is what manhood is!
So this is why they strut up and down in their white angel-
suits! They hide their women away for this! For this they worry
about the honour of their women as we worry about food for
our children! They have an ugly tap which needs to be near

something warm before it can jerk out its sticky poison." They allowed me the luxury of feeling complete contempt for their need, for their whole sex. They were like nasty children who needed to piss badly. Usually afterwards I only had to wash my outside.

'But with Dr Duke it was different. Much worse. You see, I respected him. I would never have bared my soul to him if I had not thought I could trust him. He was almost like a priest to me.

'Anyway, St Thérèse, Dr Duke went over to the video machine and put a tape in. Then he came back to where I was sitting watching him. He undid his flies and took out his thing. He turned to the television and zapped it on. First, for a moment, we were watching "Golden Girls". I like the grand-mother and, despite the sight of him there with his thing out, I was trying to think about what grandmother was saying. But then the picture changed and I saw a fat white man on the screen, his thing big and near the camera, with girls who could have been Thais or Filipinas writhing all over him, kissing the big thing and making him moan. Dr Duke was watching the video, playing with his thing, which was very long, but soft. He would look over at me from time to time, hissing, "I'm gong to get me some, I'm going to get me some. My tight little slut sitting like a good girl with her ironing! I'm going to get me some!" He fast-forwarded the video and I almost wanted to laugh because the old man looked so funny when he started to lie on top of one of the women. His fat bottom just went up and down like a clockwork toy. Then he returned the video to normal where the man was standing and a young girl was kneeling in front of him and he was doing it into her mouth, holding on to her ears. He watched that for a minute or two and then he came over to me. His thing was still not hard. They need to be, St Thérèse. It's a biological thing. Unless they are they can't do it. I thought you ought to know. He stood me up across the ironing board from him and lay his thing down on it. "Bow down and kiss it, then take it in your mouth until it's hard! Go on, Miss Green Card, Miss Third World Guilt, Miss Abused Teacher, Miss Virgin and Martyr Among the Pots and Pans, get down onto it and show me what you're good for!" He grabbed me by the shoulder with one hand, then put his other round the back of my head, forcing me towards him. I bowed down. My nose was full of snot from weeping and I wondered if I could wipe it on the shirt I was ironing. I saw the thing against the gingham ironing-board cover. I did not think. I had the iron in my right hand and suddenly he was screaming. He let me go and tried to pull the iron off his thing. But I was pushing down in the way I sometimes have to on badly creased cotton. I am sure you know all about ironing cotton from your work in the convent. It can be very stubborn. Anyway, I think I may have been screaming too. He started lashing out at my face like a drowning cat. I drew back and he was screaming on the floor. On the video screen the girl was fighting to get away from the man's huge thing but he was holding her tightly by the ears, growling "All of it, bitch!" I looked at the girl, then I looked down at Dr Duke writhing on the floor, screaming.

'I turned off the iron, went into the bathroom and washed my face. I then returned to the room where Dr Duke was. I telephoned for an ambulance. Dr Duke's Rolex was on the table. I looked at it. I suppose that I was trying to distract myself from the sight of Dr Duke on the floor. I did not want to look at him as I thought it might make me feel pity. The watch was such a small thing. I remember that I saw each link of the bracelet and imagined the things just one link would buy for us back home. I saw the tiny gold needle of the second hand and heard it tinkle on to the tiny scales of a Manila jeweler. Dr Duke continued to scream but I thought I could hear the Rolex ticking.

'I am still shocked at myself. I, who hate to see anything in pain, who would pray for the goats of Arabia with their throats cut thrashing about on the ground, did not feel an ounce of pity for Dr Duke screaming on the floor. I could not be moved by what I had done with my hot iron, just as he could not be moved by what could be done with his ticking Rolex. I know it is wrong and unchristian and diminishes me but this is an eye for an eye world, an old testament world. Only from the poor are the turning of cheeks, the spreading of legs, the smiling beatitudes of passivity, expected.

'Anyway, St Thérèse, you can imagine the rest, I think. They took him to St Vincent's hospital and I telephoned Mrs Duke to tell her there had been an accident. I said he had been ironing a pair of trousers and had somehow burnt himself. Mrs Duke said, "He's been WHAT? He's never ironed anything *in his life*!" But it is strange how things work out, St Thérèse. Almost miraculous in a way, because when Dr Duke came round that is exactly what he told his wife! What else could he tell her?

'But even though our lies coincided Mrs Duke did not believe it. I think, perhaps, she discovered the video in the machine and suspected the truth. On her return from her visit to St Vincent's she took me aside and told me to pack my things. She would give me a month's salary. I just nodded. I had been looking after the children, watching the boys zapping the television channels, daydreaming. I often do this, St Thérèse. All the time in the Dukes' house as I dust or tidy away the children's toys and clothes, I will look at an object and see its cost transferred to my family. I sometimes like to imagine that I have a machine in my hands like they have to close the drapes or change the channel on the television. But instead of changing channels my machine transfers the value of objects across continents. Why does somebody not invent such a machine? I could zap Dr Duke's Rolex and lift our family up. St Thérèse, I know there is no magic machine. But I have you, St Thérèse. You must be my magic machine.

'So, St Thérèse, what I need more than anything is a new job. Please help me to find a new job. You have helped me before. Please do it again. Intercede with Jesus and His Holy Mother for me! Ask them also to stay the hand of the US

Immigration men. They do not understand the problems of the poor. They will put me on a plane back to Manila. If they do that my life is finished, the lives of all who depend on me are finished.'

Dolores looked hard into the unblinking eyes of St Thérèse. Then she stood up and walked towards the high altar, on which stood the tabernacle. Her shoes clicked on the marble and the sound echoed around the cathedral. She began walking on tip-toe. Then she bowed her head, daring neither to look at the tabernacle nor consider the Godhead within it, hidden in the form of bread and wine. Usually Dolores only approached the saints, who then approached God on her behalf, because she did not feel worthy to approach Him directly. But today she was desperate.

'Sweet Jesus, I am sure St Thérèse has passed on my plea to you by now. I am so sorry to keep bothering you all. It would be OK if I were good myself, but you know what a wicked sinner I am. But you were friends with Mary Magdalen. I am a poor girl, Jesus. One of millions in my country. Our poverty forces us into sin. We give up our homes, our honour and our purity so that our children may eat. In Japan, Arabia, England and America, we marry, maid, teach and are prostituted. This is the fate of the poor and powerless. *Dear Lord, Father of the Poor, forgive me and help me to find a new job.'*

Dolores repeated the last sentence of her prayer again and again, kneeling at the altar rails. She did not immediately take notice of the tumult at the back of the cathedral, the voices raised, the winding of cameras, the flash-guns popping. The repeated last sentence brought tears to her eyes once more. She stared through her tears at the curtains of the tabernacle, sending a beam of pleading as strong as anything the Duke children zapped at their computer, through the silk curtain and the metal doors and the chalices, to the Godhead hidden within.

Then, quite suddenly, she heard the noise. Robbed of concentration, her thoughts pushed back to her suitcase in the Dukes' lobby, Dolores stood up. She genuflected in front of the

altar and turned to leave the cathedral. She tip-toed back up
the central aisle, seeing through the gloom a scene of mayhem.
A woman was walking towards her, on her knees. Behind the
woman, a jostling group of people, pushing, straining, using
their elbows and whispered shrieks, tried to get a better look.
Dolores stopped when she realised that the woman on her
knees was Imelda Marcos. Her arms were outstretched and it
seemed to Dolores that those arms were coming to enfold her,
while they kept at bay the wild people behind. A glittering
rosary was hanging from the white-gloved fingers of her right
hand. Imelda shuffled towards Dolores, her lips moving. Tears
had leaked over the barricades of her mascara and were
coursing black down both cheeks. Dolores stared at the apparition. She had stopped in the centre of the aisle, eyes wide, her
head full of the glittering celebrity on her knees before her.
Imelda seemed to be looking at Dolores, begging her forgiveness. For the briefest of moments Dolores thought that this
was how her prayer was going to be answered. Imelda Marcos
had been made aware by St Thérèse of her crimes against her,
her family and all the millions of struggling Filipinos. She
would stop in front of Dolores and beg her forgiveness,
perhaps give her one of the stones from her brooch, her rosary
or her flashing ear-rings.

A perfume of roses filled the air. Dolores was practically
fainting away from the perfume, from the feeling that here she
was in the middle of another miracle, beyond any chronicled in
her Dictionary of the Saints.

A thought came, a thought that she knew had been given
her by sweet St Thérèse. After Imelda had wept apologies and
promised her a job and the making of restitution to the
Filipino people she, Dolores, would lift Imelda to her feet
and together they would go back to the altar rails to weep tears
of joy, to pray in tongues of burning gratitude. Imelda would
auction off her baubles. She would take the magic remote
machine and zap the buildings she owned in New York so that

their value was transferred to the poor in the Philippines. The buildings would be dissolved. Each brick, window frame, floor tile, light fitting, door, mirror and drape would fly up high into the air, dance gloriously across the ether and softly fall on her homeland. Houses for the poor would be formed by these things. Schools and clinics and workshops click into place.

The New York skyline would look no different. The missing buildings would not be missed. Rather, more sun would beam down into the cold canyons, warming the city's stony heart. From the sites of the buildings springs would flow that would cure the sick. But more than that, just as the scales had fallen from the eyes of Imelda, so all in New York would see that dollars were not worth chasing. Only Beatitudes were worth effort.

Dolores smiled through tears of joy at Imelda shuffling towards her. Only twelve feet separated them now. Dolores imagined once again what she would do when Imelda arrived at her feet. She would reach down towards Imelda and offer her arms to her, would get down and enfold the penitent, would lift her up, cradling her as she had cradled for so long the babies of strangers; tell her that everything was all right, heaven hers.

But then a bodyguard elbowed Dolores out of the way. She was pushed against a pew and saw that Imelda's eyes had not moved. They wept still, but their gaze had not been fixed upon Dolores at all, but the golden tabernacle on the altar.

Dolores sat down heavily in a pew. Imelda shuffled on past her. Cameramen ran down the side aisles of the cathedral, jumped over pews as if they were so many hurdles in a race, shooting picture after picture as they went. She heard the cameras winding on, saw intense white flashes behind her closed eyelids. The flashes turned into suns shining down on Sebastian as he foraged with his stick on Smoky Mountain, a cloth over his nose. He looked up at the suns, then out at her. The cloth fell from his face and she saw that he was screaming.

When Dolores, anxious to awake from her nightmare, opened her eyes, she saw Imelda Marcos kneeling in front of the tabernacle on the high altar of St Patrick's cathedral – where hides the God of the Poor – thanking Him for the miracle.

Guest Workers

Walking back to the huts from the tap outside the Islamic Centre, two of the three Filipino guest workers kept looking over their shoulders at approaching cars. None stopped. None ever stopped.

Neither did the pair wonder why they continued to glance uselessly around. Each time their eyes caught headlights looking straight ahead, a small humiliation reddened ears and necks, and a memory of cars and trucks along some track at home impinged – cars that stopped and let them ride. Then the blush would fade with the retreating rear-view lights of the car and they would continue their walk thinking of tracks at home and small kindnesses, kindnesses which, in the foreign dark, they endowed with an idealised sunset-pink glow.

The group held their tablets of Dettol soap and walked in silence. The cicadas chirped from the raggedy jungle close to the road and each of the men was lost in thought.

Manolo watched his left flip-flop and walked with a slight limp. It was coming apart – the rubber stud that held the pink plastic thong to fit between his toes kept coming away from the sole, the hole having widened and perished from use. He did not want to buy another pair. He had worried about it for days. While mixing cement or slapping it between cinder-blocks, he would find himself thinking not of his work but of himself going into the market and bargaining for a new pair. The trouble was that here the shopkeepers were too rich to bargain. He fantasised about the shopkeepers laughing at him in a hundred different ways.

Then he had thought of another approach. He would take all his savings out from under the water tank near the hut and waft the notes in front of the shopkeepers. That would show them he was a big man. He would have to pay the full price but his pride would return from the market intact. But always he came back to the conclusion that a new pair of flip-flops was not budgeted.

He wished as he walked that he had picked up the discarded pair he had seen down by the river the previous Friday. But last Friday his own had been all right. Manolo was coming to the end of the fourth pair of flip-flops bought away from home. Each pair he bought cost him, with much bargaining, two-and-a-half times what they would cost at home. True, he still had his leather sandals, the ones he had arrived in, with their thick rubber tyre-tread soles, but they were stored in a plastic bag in the hut and would not be used until he walked back to the airport – a new cassette-player wrapped in a sarong to protect it from the dust, a cassette-player with auto-reverse and Dolby and a built-in microphone – back to freedom.

Next to Manolo, Angelo wondered why he had come from his poor village to be poorer in this rich slice of oil land. At home he had his hashish and his dreams and his friends. Here he could only see himself, miserable, when compared with the riches of everyone around. It was harder to be poor in a rich country, painful to be the minority on foot. At home, well in the majority, he could join the others in hooting at the Mercedes cars which corrupt practices had procured.

He took out a Marlboro from his sarong and lit it, thinking of the advertisement. Instead of the cowboy Angelo saw himself upon the horse; the horses behind were ridden by his friends. They smoked and whooped and galloped down the fledgling sugar cane of the landowner who had grown fat on their toil, and who, when they had proved surplus to his requirements, had seduced them into paying him for a job in this rich country. He saw the horses galloping to the landowner's hacienda. The white Mercedes stood parked before the door. Tony, his friend, aimed a gob of spit at the windscreen of the car and hit it. The guard got up from the step and aimed his rifle but Angelo was faster and killed the man with one blast from his rifle, standing in the stirrups to take aim. The landowner, fat and moustached, ran on to the veranda shouting. Another shot caught him between the eyes.

They dismounted and went in search of the man's wife and daughters. On the stairs they shot out the face of the portrait of Marcos. They pawed and guffawed at the bejewelled cleavage of his wife. In their cowboy boots they stood on the deep rug of the landing and heard the whimperings of the women. Without care or compassion Angelo kicked open the bedroom door and strutted into the room like a Hollywood hero. The women screamed and swooned. A scent of perfume filled the air . . .

Abdul Kadir was the only one of the group who did not look out for lifts. He walked ahead of his two companions, the small Chinese towel he had used to dry his hair wrapped around his neck like a scarf, a small cap on his head. He was aware of the cars passing and of their dust and the smell of the Dettol mixing with his new sweat. And, behind this, another smell, one that he had begun to believe he had always smelt and would always smell; a smell that was the trademark of this country: the burning jungle. Everywhere it burnt. Looking up to his left, upon a hillside, the jungle burnt. Tall trees turned to skeletons before his eyes, trees that had taken a hundred years to grow were crackling out a death chant nearby.

He hardly thought of this either. The burning jungle in this tiny oil-rich country was as much a part of life and routine as the fast-passing cars which never stopped. The jungle burning had been his first sight of the country as the plane approached from Mindanao. The smell had greeted him with the surly gestures of the Chinese agent's man who had collected them and dumped them in their squalid workcamp without a tap. Now he inhaled the scent of burning wood with joy. To these pampered people the jungle was a garden, a pretty backdrop to their sprawling villas. He knew they wept and grieved to see it burning up. He did not grieve. He wanted their country to become a desert pock-marked with the totems of black tree-trunks.

For these people had sold their souls to the Devil of possessions. These people were not Muslims. In his village, or so his ideal memory told him, the poorest man would welcome any stranger to his house. No one ever passed by a walking man. He, poor fool, had thought that in a rich country Muslims would bestow their wealth on everyone. How naïve he had been! The richer, the harder. The more blessed the less likely to bless. Only the poor were truly generous. The poor had no fear. The poor knew how you hurt because they hurt also.

Abdul Kadir did not smoke or drink. He prayed on the mat outside the hut he shared with Angelo and Manolo, but never did he go to the mosque. The Call to Prayer from the concrete mosque near the work-camp, the mosque he had helped build, did not move him. He was a prisoner, though he had done nothing wrong, and prisoners do not pray with their captors.

All three men felt they had been tricked. Agents had promised them a salary back home which had not materialised. In return they had promised the agent a fixed sum, had signed and had witnessed their promise to pay a certain sum each month. At home, they knew, their families were hostages to that promise. But when they arrived in the oil-rich country, the agents laughed when they mentioned the terms they had come expecting and said they would be paid only a third of the amount. Abdul Kadir had gone to the muezzin in the main mosque to ask for his help but the man had refused to even speak to him. The police laughed in his face. Then he had not been paid for three months. Letters had come from both wife and agent begging and threatening and pleading. Then the three men begged and threatened and pleaded whenever they met the agent's man. He shrugged.

When they had been building the mosque, Abdul Kadir had had to drive down to the beach to collect sand to mix with cement for the concrete. Piles of sand had been taken from the beach and left for the rains to leach out the salt. He had started to ignore the salt-free piles and taken sand fresh from the sea. He hoped that the mosque would fall down upon the heads of the hypocrites.

Manolo started to sing a song: 'Sherry! Sherry! Baby! / Love me like no other! / I will be your lover! / Sherry! Sherry! Baby!'

'Stop!' Abdul Kadir snapped without turning. He scowled at the two shadows behind him.

'Why stop? You say stop! I like songs, man! Songs good, man!' But Manolo did not continue his song. He just whistled a few more bars to save face and was silent.

'What you do first when you get back home?' Abdul Kadir heard Manolo ask Angelo.

'You know that, man!' answered Angelo.

'Say it again!'

'I take taxi from the airport. No service taxi. Only me. I drink from bottle of Napoleon Five Star same like the Chinese drink. I wave to all the pretty girls. When I get to the village I go straight to Rosie's place and I . . .'

Both Manolo and Angelo inhaled noisily, then shouted to the star-full sky, 'THE GIRLS! MAKE THE GIRLS SCREAM!'

A peal of laughter followed the loud exclamation and then slowly died into the silence.

'Hey, AK!' shouted Angelo. 'What you do first?'

Abdul Kadir did not answer them. He knew what he would do, though, and he told himself, 'Buy a gun and a box of bullets and kill them all.'

Sharon saw them in the car headlights, three pencil-slim men walking along the road in a line. She often saw them on her way back from the hospital to her lodgings in the hospital compound. Sometimes when she passed they were still wash-

ing themselves at the tap outside the Islamic Centre; at other
times they were turning off the road, having completed their
walk of a mile-and-a-half, making towards the group of little
huts at the top of the hill. She had often felt for them and
thought how unfair it was that they should have to come this
far in order to wash. Usually she thought when she saw them
how blessed she was in comparison. True, she had ended up
a volunteer in a country that should not have volunteers;
received a pittance serving a people who could have afforded
to pay. But, seeing these unfortunates, also expatriates,
buoyed her up for, if one keeps one's eyes half open, it is not
difficult to find people less fortunate than oneself.

Two of the figures turned and she saw the blank stares as
she passed them. A twinge of guilt pricked her, and she
wondered if tonight she should stop. But, she told herself,
they were a good two-thirds of the way back home. Besides it
was not the custom to stop.

Then, two hundred yards past the group, she looked in her
driving mirror and found herself stopping. She reversed
until she saw the three shadows heading up. She reached
over and opened the passenger door, unlocking the back door
too.

'Want a lift?' she asked.

Three blank faces gazed back at her and she felt suddenly
very foolish.

Angelo came to the open door and looked in. He smiled
and then his face suddenly became blank again. He tossed his
head questioningly as a horse will when the bridle is put over
his face.

'Do you want a lift?' Sharon asked again.

Angelo turned and spoke to Manolo and Abdul Kadir. At
once the two were sitting in the back while Angelo sat in
front, next to her.

Sharon crashed the gears and started the car.

'What your name?' asked Angelo, lighting a Marlboro.

'Sharon.' She frowned and pretended to be concentrating on the road.

Manolo began singing the song.

'Yes, like that,' said Sharon.

'You married?' asked Angelo. She saw that he was leaning far back in the seat, his legs crossed, his face towards her with the cigarette burning like a joss stick before the altar of his leer.

'No, I work here – at the hospital.'

She saw the men's huts on the hillside in the distance. She slowed down, then stopped.

'How you know we live here?' asked Angelo.

'I have passed you before.'

'But you don't stop?'

'No.' She tossed her long hair back then with her left hand pushed some sweat-caught wisps and teased them back. 'Sorry.' She laughed.

Angelo started talking to Abdul Kadir and Manolo in the back. She thought how ugly their language was, how unpleasant the smell from the still-burning cigarette. 'Well, here you are!' she said to herself and to them.

A heated argument was taking place. Then she heard the car door open behind her and, looking through the open window, saw Abdul Kadir standing next to her.

'I am Muslim,' said Abdul Kadir.

'What do you mean?' Sharon asked but he did not answer her.

'You really should go now,' she told them.

'Drive us more!' said Angelo.

'Sherry! Sherry! Baby! / Love me like no other! / I will be your lover! / Sherry! Sherry! Baby . . .' sang Manolo. He reached and grabbed Angelo's cigarette, lit one of his own and sprawled across both seats behind her.

'Look! I've brought you home! I've given you a lift! Get out!' And she hated her voice as it came out broken and falsetto and spoilt.

'Drive us more!' repeated Angelo.

So this is how it feels, she thought.

In the early morning Manolo and Angelo returned to the huts. Manolo kicked Abdul Kadir awake and said to him:

'You missed good time!'

'What happened?' Abdul Kadir asked him.

'Many bad things. Look what we have.' And he showed Abdul Kadir a suitcase.

'So what happens now? The police will catch you.'

'Now we rob a bank and go in jungle to border!' replied Angelo, lighting another Marlboro with a pretty, very feminine, gold lighter.

The German Cuckoo

In 1952 the Queen got crowned on the pricey little box in the corner of the Rudges' lounge. This, in Benson's eyes, was a moment of great moment, for he had proved beyond all doubt that the Rudges – a secretive family who belonged to the Church Army and could often be seen marching up the road in uniform carrying oddly shaped suitcases – were in fact owners of only the second television in the avenue.

Usually, of course, the big H-shaped aerial attached to the chimney of a house told Benson that inside dwelled a family for whom Snakes and Ladders, learning long bits of poetry, boring conversations, were things of the past. The odd thing about the Rudges was that there was no aerial in sight. Only when they generously opened up their lounge for the curious to view the coronation did all stand flickeringly revealed.

'Of course I knew all the time,' said Benson to Eric, his best friend – despite the fact that Benson found Eric trying. 'Didn't I tell you that something was going on in their lounge? They've probably got the aerial in the loft.'

'Why?' asked Eric.

'Well, it's obvious, isn't it?' replied Benson. 'For a start television is worldly. If the vicar knew he'd be round. It steals time from the Church Army. And for a finish, televisions cost an arm and a leg. They should be sending their spare money to China.'

Benson stopped to receive the acclaim he felt he deserved for his revelations, but Eric said nothing. 'Also,' Benson continued after a pause, 'there's a little matter of the cost of a television licence. Anyway, they kill conversation, Dad says. It's a good job you don't have one, Eric. You probably wouldn't ever say another word.'

Then Eric, imitating his dad who was a lecturer in teaching, bit his lip, rubbed his chin and said, 'That depends . . .'

'What's that supposed to mean?' asked Benson.

'That depends . . .' repeated Eric.

Benson biffed Eric on the arm and stalked off. He bounced his ball off the Rudges' wall for a few minutes, hoping that the Rudges might repeat their invitation to come in and watch their television. But the lace curtains remained unruffled and Benson kicked his ball up the avenue where he started bouncing it against Mr Johnson's wall. But he knew that was hopeless. Though Mr Johnson had a great big tell-tale H on his chimney, he was away.

Eric caught up with Benson. 'That's no good. He's in Germany,' he said.

'I know that, Eric!' replied Benson, tripping Eric up. 'In fact, I think I told you that some time ago.'

'No you didn't,' replied Eric, who had not yet learnt that arguing with Benson was not the best way to avoid scabs on knees acquired as a result of being barged to the pavement by the bigger, fatter boy. 'Mrs Eccles round the corner told Miss Lynch and Miss Lynch told my mum.'

Benson nodded inwardly. 'What's he doing in Germany, do you think? The war's over. We won.' He strafed Eric with automatic arm fire, but Eric did not co-operate by dying like a Jerry. Instead he said, 'My mum says he's got friends there.'

Benson was shocked. The Germans had been responsible for Benson spending his formative years eking out a tiny ration of sweets, eating hateful dripping toast, drinking cod-liver oil. He'd only been let off the hook by the crowning of the Queen. Benson would never forgive the Germans for those early years. Never.

'He can't have friends in Germany! That's impossible!' said Benson.

'That depends . . .' said Eric.

*

It was not until the following March that Benson noticed signs of life from Mr Johnson's house. The curtains, closed since the previous May, were open. Then in the evening he saw a 1952 Standard Vanguard sitting in the pathway of the house. He left his grammar book on the table, seized his ball and trotted up the avenue to investigate further.

After three bounces he put plan A into operation and gave the ball a great heave which sent it over the fence at the side of Mr Johnson's house into his back garden. Wearing a look of great misery, he then rang the bell, confident that Mr Johnson would answer and give him the scoop on his nefarious activities in Germany.

Benson was shocked when a slim young woman answered the door. She had blonde hair, tightly woven into plaits gathered about the top of her head.

Benson looked at the apparition admiringly, finding time in the midst of his confusion to think how like the Holy Picture of Saint Ursula, kept in his Sunday Missal, she was. 'Er . . .' he began. 'Er . . . can I have my ball back, please. It's gone into your back garden.'

'Please?' she asked.

'Please can I have my ball back er . . . please?'

The woman looked confused. She gripped the front door, seemed about to close it. Then she made a patting gesture with her thin hand to Benson and said, 'A minute.' She disappeared and he saw Mr Johnson striding down the hall towards him.

'Hello, Martin. It's nice to see you again. You've grown.'

'Yes, I have. Mum took me to the shoe shop and Mr Tasker put my feet in the X-ray machine. My toes, he said, are beginning to curl against the end of my shoes. But Mum said I'd have to wait for a new pair because they cost an arm and a leg.'

'What can I do for you?'

'My ball's gone into your back garden.'

Mr Johnson nodded. His hair glistened becomingly with Brylcreem, a luxury which Mum would never allow him. 'Put tap water on it,' she told him. But water glistened only for a while, then dried.

Mr Johnson spoke in German to the woman who had come to the door. She disappeared, reappearing a moment later with his ball in one hand and a sweet in the other. She gave Benson the ball and then held out the sweet. 'For you, little boy,' she said.

Benson took the sweet and thanked the woman. She stroked his hair.

'Right then. Bye,' said Benson.

'My name is Anna,' said the woman.

'Yes,' said Benson.

Benson did not manage to locate Eric until the following evening because Eric had been sent to bed early for blotting his sister's gymslip with Quink Radiant Blue.

'Mr Johnson's got a German staying with him,' said Benson.

'Has he?'

'Yes. It makes you wonder. I mean, Sister Paul told us we had to forgive our enemies til 70 times 7 and 70 times 7 is er . . . 490. Now I'm sure I've had to eat at least 700 times 7 pieces of dripping toast in my time and it was all the Germans' fault. If it hadn't been for them I'd have had butter. It's a bit of a problem.'

But Eric wasn't listening. 'Dad threw my Osmiroid fountain pen in the fire. He says I'm not ready for it,' he said.

'She gave me a sweet,' said Benson. 'Still she's barking up the wrong tree if she thinks she can buy me off with sweets. Anyway, it was marzipan. It went in no time at all.'

'Dad says I've got to write with a pencil from now on. I don't know what Miss Dowland will say,' commented Eric, locked in his own tragedy, seeing his pen curling over a coal, sizzling, weeping bakelite tears like a lost soul.

Benson left Eric to his gloomy meditations. In the weeks that followed, he took to playing with his ball outside Mr Johnson's house. He did not know quite why he did it, though Eric thought that the television inside had a lot to do with it.

One day he saw the curtains rustle and Anna opened the door and beckoned Benson to her. 'Come!' she called.

Benson looked around, pointing to himself before approaching.

'Good night, Martin.' Benson did not comment, even though it was hardly yet evening. 'I have one gift for you.'

'A gift? For me? You shouldn't have,' he trotted out in his practised manner.

'Yes. One gift from Germany.'

Anna held out a piece of wood which, upon closer inspection, Benson saw was a whistle, the end carved into the shape of a bird's head. Anna put the whistle to her lips. 'Hear!' she commanded.

Benson heard a clear note, then a second, lower one when Anna placed her finger over the single stop behind the bird's head. 'That's the sound a cuckoo makes!' said Benson, thrilled.

Anna nodded and gave him the whistle. He thanked her effusively, wondering why she had numbers on the inside of her thin arm. He walked home making cuckoo noises, thinking about the numbers. Probably Anna had trouble remembering her co-op number. Mr Johnson would be angry if he was diddled out of his divvy.

Throughout that evening the Bensons' lounge played host to Benson indulging his new skill at cuckoo cries until Dad said he thought that was probably enough. Reluctantly, Benson laid aside the whistle and started writing his name on his arm with his Bic Click.

'What are you doing?' asked Dad.

'Writing my name. What's our 'phone number, Dad?'

'Why?'

'Anna, Mr Johnson's friend, has numbers on her arm.'

Dad looked sad and told Benson that was because she had been in a concentration camp.

'What's a concentration camp, Dad?'

'It's too old for you,' said Dad. 'Why don't you play with your cuckoo whistle?'

'Right-ho.'

In bed that night Benson wondered about concentration camps. Sister Paul of the Cross had accused Benson of lacking concentration. A camp was where rough boys went . . . 'So a concentration camp must be a place where you learn concentration. Poor Anna!'

During the night Benson rolled over on to his cuckoo whistle, taken to bed with him, the sheet folded just under its beak; but which had worked its way down the bed as Benson tossed and turned.

The following evening he went up the road to serenade Anna with his cuckoo whistle. She heard him and came out of the front door. They played ball for a while. Then Benson asked, 'What was the concentration camp like?'

'Again,' she said.

Benson repeated his question.

Anna's face changed. She stared at him as Our Lady of Sorrows stared at him from the wall of his class at the convent, her heart pierced by a knife.

'It wasn't very nice then?' he asked.

'It wasn't very nice,' she said.

Benson nodded. 'Dad keeps saying I should go to Catholic Camp. It's run by the St Vincent de Paul Society. But Mum says some of the boys who go are a bit rough. I'm really enjoying my cuckoo whistle. You can't get them here for love nor money. I'm going to take it to school tomorrow to show the teacher.'

Anna smiled at Benson sadly, then her hands sandwiched his cheeks and she kissed him lightly on the forehead. The place burnt. He smelled her soap and saw the tears on her face. She turned without a word and disappeared through the front door.

Another H-shaped aerial went up in the avenue, atop Eric's chimney. Benson began to frequent Eric's house with clockwork-regularity to watch the miraculous invention in the corner of the lounge. When it got late he would sit on the carpet in the gap between the sofa and the sideboard, hoping that the adults would forget he was there. He was in his hiding place when he saw a programme which told him what concentration camps were.

The next day he was back outside Anna's house announcing the approach of spring, blowing his whistle lustily. Anna did not come out. He kept at it. At last Mr Johnson came out and told him to stop it. Anna was trying to work. The sound of the cuckoo upset her.

'But a cuckoo's supposed to make you happy! Sister Stanislaus says so. People write to the papers when they hear one, they're so happy!' protested Benson.

Mr Johnson told him how the cuckoo takes over the nests of smaller, gentler birds, and throws the young to the ground. 'I think Anna thinks of that. I've got a cuckoo clock and I've had to put sticky tape over the door. You don't mind, do you? We're both in the same boat in a way. I used to like my cuckoo clock.'

Benson said he didn't mind. He jittered on the spot.

'One thing, Martin. Anna's going to have a baby. You can tell your mum that if you like. You're the first to know,' said Mr Johnson.

'Mum, guess what?' said Benson portentously.

'What?' asked Mum, as she poured out Scotch pancake batter on to the hissing griddle.

'Anna's going to have a baby.'

'Well it's about time! A baby's probably just what she needs.'

'Yes.'

He watched the batter sizzling, the bubbles forming as the little round blotches on the black griddle browned and made his mouth water. Then his eyes took in the oven below the range.

Stephen O'Neill had offered him his King Conker and a Tom Merry Annual in exchange for his cuckoo whistle. If the offer still held, and if he could get him to add his enamel Flying Scotsman badge to the trade, he would swap it in the playground during playtime. Mum was turning the Scotch pancakes over. He ran over to her weeping, burying his face in her tummy, using his head to butt her away from the oven.

A Day by the Sea with Mr Shukry

Mr Shukry awoke to the sound of the Arabian Sea. He listened to the unkind breaking waves roaring with laughter and then inhaling noisily, retreating across the pebbles to prepare for another guffaw.

'Why must you always laugh at me? It is both ill-bred and misanthropic,' Mr Shukry told the sea in English. He always spoke to himself and inanimate objects in English. That way the other teachers could not understand. With a sigh of 'Ya Allah!' he pulled his heavy head from the pillow, manoeuvring himself to a sitting position. Then he scratched at his ankles. The sand flies had bitten him during the night as they did every night.

'You might have given me respite today. I have enough troubles today without you adding to them,' Mr Shukry told the long-gone insects.

He listened to the headmaster gargling in the waterless bathroom next to his room. Soon the headmaster would call his staff to morning prayers, a green turban wrapped around his head.

'Come on, Mr Shukry. It is better to pray than to sleep,' he told his still-dozing side. With difficulty he got off the low bed and pulled himself into his white dish-dash. He performed his ablutions from an enamel bowl, thinking of the visit of the inspector and of Ziggerzig on the Nile Delta where at this moment his family would still be curled in sleep.

'Sleep, my dears,' he told them. 'For you Shukry has ventured across the wide world in order to earn you the little extras that the bounteous Nile cannot provide for those of her sons who are landless. When Shukry embraced the flame of education, did he not burn his hand? But sleep, my dears! Only remember your father sweating blood for you in oil-rich Ras Al Surra.'

The gravel voice of the headmaster called him to prayer. Mr Shukry shuffled into his pink flip-flops and joined the line of teachers, their faces towards the rising sun and the dark legions of dunes between them and Mecca.

As he bowed, knelt and stood in prayer, he noticed the track that led circuitously from Tiwi to the tarmacked road that began forty miles away. That track would bring the inspector. And Mr Shukry prayed for himself. He prayed that the inspector, an Englishman whose reputation for severity to-wards Egyptian teachers was legendary throughout the Eastern Region, would look kindly upon him. 'For, though I am in prison here,' prayed Mr Shukry, 'a eunuch away from Leila, a slave to a barbarian people . . . For the sake of my family and my half-built house in Ziggerzig, I beseech You to grant me a good report from the English inspector.'

And he added with passion: 'Remember Suez, my God!'

The inspector of English language for the Eastern Region of Ras Al Surra was greatly looking forward to his trip to Tiwi and Mr Shukry.

Since his arrival in the country two months before, not a day, not an hour, had passed without the inspector wanting to pick up his suitcase and run away home. The weather, the lack of electricity, the inefficiency, the books he delivered and which mysteriously disappeared, the feeling that he was completely unable to function and do a decent job, had bubbled up in his brain, turning what had looked like a challenge in London into a cross of impossible weight in Ras Al Surra. The English teacher in Mintarib who could not speak, read or write English and had succeeded in teaching only, 'Go home, Johnnie!' and 'For you, best price!' to his students, had put him into a depression which had lasted for weeks. Dull nights alone in fly-blown guest houses gave ample opportunity for his negative feelings to combine into a thick poisonous soup, inedible, but easy enough to be eaten by.

He felt, as he aimed the temperamental Landrover towards Tiwi, that he was more than ready for a day by the sea with Mr Shukry.

In the inspector's mind, Mr Shukry had stood out from the start. He was, the inspector recalled, about five-foot-three in his winkle pickers, had the regulation Egyptian moustache – always in process of growth but never allowed to reach full maturity. His eyes were small and twinkling, his hair layered like a grandstand, with the texture of steel wool. He carried his head upright upon a pear-shaped body made of beans and rice.

But it was the man's energy that had made an indelible initial impression on the inspector. In a lazy place, Mr Shukry bounced, twinkled and flashed.

The inspector had only met him on one occasion. He had just arrived in Ras Al Surra and, along with the three other English inspectors, was giving a Training Workshop for the teachers prior to the start of the new school year. It had been held during the month of Ramadan, the Islamic fast period, and the teachers were either fasting or giving convincing impersonations of self-denial. They lounged at their desks and fidgeted as the inspector described new methods of getting conversations going in class; they yawned, scratched and watched the clock throughout his introduction to phonetics. Some completely gave up the ghost and lay sprawled and snoring as the day neared its end and the inspector tried to raise some enthusiasm with a discussion on the psychology of language learners.

But not Mr Shukry. He had sat erect at his desk, eyes twinkling. When the inspector asked for ideas, it was Mr Shukry alone who shot up a hairy hand to volunteer answers.

'The main thing I think is that we go near our boys and say the sentence again and again. Only this way can we assure the boys of a good English saying.'

'Very true. Very true,' the inspector had said, cheered.

'And, if I may to continue,' continued Mr Shukry, 'I think that we all know from our reading of Pestalozzi and Mr Froebel and Mrs Maria Montessori and the great Briton Lord Bertrand Russell, we, because being teachers, must love the boys.'

'Mmmmm. Yes. Er . . .' opined the inspector.

'And we because being teachers must open the door and the windows to the classroom and pull in the wind of the world to the small air of the classroom. Then it is imperative that we show the wind of the world to the boys and show the boys to the wind of the world and say, "Here, boys! This is the world's wind! Smell it! Taste it! Feel it!"'

'Thank you, Mr Er . . . That gives us much food for thought. Thank you.'

From then on the Training Workshop became a dialogue between the inspector and Mr Shukry alone. The inspector felt happy, fulfilled and useful. Mr Shukry became a green sprouting branch announcing spring while all around the sleeping trees of winter snored on.

Since then, experience had made him forget that spring could come. He felt that he was becoming cold and hard. He shouted at teachers; he walked out of schools in a huff; he wrote lethal memos to the Education Office in the capital; and he wrote to his former boss at the Quick School of Languages in London asking for his old job back.

Mr Shukry was his last chance.

After prayers the headmaster approached Mr Shukry and said, 'Don't forget, Mr Shukry, my English teacher, today the inspector is coming.'

Mr Shukry smiled wanly and fled back to his room. Every day for the last fortnight the headmaster had warned him about the coming visit and regaled him with tales told by arriving camel trains and coastal sailing vessels of the mayhem being wrought throughout the Eastern Region by the new English inspector. And, as he told the stories of teachers hounded out of the Kingdom for inefficiency, a smile played around his thick, too-red lips. Mr Shukry's nightmare of being repatriated tearfully with his 'Long March' suitcase, and his return to Ziggerzig and ignominious unemployment, had been daily fuelled by this. It had driven any kindly memories he might have had of the inspector from his sun-battered brain.

Back in his room again he opened the tin wardrobe and removed a bowl of oranges he had been saving for some time. He began polishing the oranges one by one. As he did so, he intoned, 'Here you are, my dear inspector. This is for you.' But then he stopped, thinking, 'Is that right?' He scrambled about for his English Grammar but it did not help him.

He tried again, 'Here you are, dear my inspector. This is for you.' Both sounded right. He replaced the oranges in the wardrobe. As he did so, a spoon banging an enamel plate summoned him to breakfast.

He rejected everything except a glass of sweet tea. Through the steam he saw Leila gesturing towards a half-completed house, part-grown children and never-departing parents. All were dependent on him. He had to stay. It was his only chance. On today rested his whole life.

Mr Shukry shook.

The inspector arrived at last. Mr Shukry gripped his hand and shook it, at the same time pulling him across the threshold of the teachers' house. Then his other hand grabbed a bottle of Pepsi Cola and thrust it into the inspector's free hand, closing his fingers around it. Then he pulled the inspector into his room.

'Nice to see you again!' exclaimed the inspector warmly.

'Thank you, dear my inspector! Now eat orange!'

He could feel his knowledge of English leaving him. He felt he was sweating letters. 'The Pepsi is not frozed . . . frozen. But what can we do? We are in prison here!'

'Never mind.'

Mr Shukry peeled the orange and the inspector ate it. Mr Shukry peeled another one.

'No, really! One is enough.'

'We do not have many things, dear my inspector, but what we have we give to you! Eat, by God!'

The inspector ate happily. It was a good orange.

Mr Shukry started to peel a third orange which the inspector refused with some vehemence. He countered, 'I have books for you, Mr Shukry. Picture dictionaries.'

'First the orange. Second the books.'

'First the books. Second the orange.'

Mr Shukry shrugged and carefully wrapped the orange in several pieces of Kleenex prior to placing it reverently on the bed. Then he said, 'Tea! Drink tea!'

An hour later the inspector was taken to see one of Mr Shukry's classes.

The school consisted of fifteen tents. Into one of these strode the inspector, followed by Mr Shukry.

The class stood up and Mr Shukry went to the front while the inspector sat at an empty desk.

'Greet our inspector, boys!' commanded Mr Shukry.

'Good morning, sir! Welcome, sir!' the boys fired back.

'Sing, boys!'

And the boys sang:

'I'm H–A–P–P–Y! I'm H–A–P–P–Y!

That means . . . that means . . .

I am happy! I am happy! To see you.'

The inspector smiled and squirmed. 'Thank you, boys . . . Oh, there's more?' And the boys started on a second verse:

'I'm G–L–A–D! I'm G–L–A–D!

That means . . . that means . . .
I am glad! I am glad! To see you.'
'Thank you again,' smiled the inspector.
'For nothing!' shot back the boys.

Then the class began in earnest and from the very first minute the inspector knew that he was not going to be disappointed. Every boy was included, enfolded in the enthusiasm of Mr Shukry. The same energy he had seen during the Workshop was evident in his teaching. Sweat trickled down his brow as he practised prepositions; moving objects around the room – under, over, in between, on top of, under other objects. The boys shot up their hands to answer, leaned far forward towards him as if they wanted to touch the round little dynamo at the front of the class.

A smile of contentment which, for once, mirrored a similar feeling deep inside, grew and flourished on the inspector's face. For the first time since his arrival in Ras Al Surra he felt needed and useful and fulfilled. Here and now, with prepositional sentences whizzing about the room like rockets, his projection of a hoped-for useful future and its reality came together at last with fine definition and in full colour.

Tears came to the inspector's eyes when a timid boy near the opening of the tent confused 'in' and 'on'. The rest of the class began a barely audible jeer which Mr Shukry silenced with a glance prior to clearing up the problem and putting the boy back on to the correct grammatical tracks. Tiwi and Mr Shukry, the inspector decided there and then, would become the object of his special attention. He would pour books and visual aids into it. He would extol its virtues throughout the Land of Ras Al Surra. To know, while touring the other hopeless schools of the Region, that Tiwi existed with its wonderful teacher, would keep away the neurotic flies of despair that had been buzzing around him for so long.

He looked forward to writing a glowing report.

*

'That was a wonderful lesson! I'm very pleased! Very pleased indeed!' said the inspector as he and Mr Shukry walked back to the teachers' house under the sweltering midday sun.

Mr Shukry stopped. 'So you do not wish to send Mr Shukry from Ras Al Surra?' he asked uncertainly.

'Send you away? The very idea!' replied the inspector vehemently.

Mr Shukry kicked at the sand as he walked, pondering the exact meaning of 'The very idea'. Did it mean, 'That's a good idea' or 'That's a bad idea'? He would have to look in his grammar book. Still, things looked hopeful, that was true. He seemed satisfied. But with the English one could never tell. After all, the forefathers of this inspector had built Suez, had used it selfishly for a century and then had bombed it when Egyptians cried, 'Enough!'

He smiled broadly and his twinkling eyes once again worked their magic on the inspector.

'Come to my cool room, dear my inspector! There are yet many oranges!' said Mr Shukry, hedging his bets.

Percy Wordsworth's First Chapter

Audrey Saunders Limited
45 Taylor Square
London WC1

3 October

Mr Percy Wordsworth
43 Scaffold Ridge
Fayers
Suffolk

Dear Mr Wordsworth,

Thank you so much for letting us have a look at your work.

We were immensely tickled by much that you sent, especially
your piece for children, *Peter Cumulus the Cloud*. Shades of
Richard Bach there, I fancy!!

You write, on the whole, pleasantly, but I do not think we can
represent you at this time. We are somewhat snowed under just
now. The storm-clouds of Thatcherism have dumped on us a
plethora of talent with nothing to do but write masterpieces.

I do hope you will not find this rejection too depressing. We
could be wrong, you know!

Yours sincerely,
Audrey Saunders

Worn out by too much sleep, standing in the bleak hall of his terraced house, Percy Wordsworth read the letter several times. It so engrossed him that he hardly noticed the cold linoleum, nor the draught coming under the door and up the trouser legs of his pyjamas. Once or twice he tried to read it as 'encouraging'; then, by changing the stress, as 'encouragingly discouraging'. But in the end he decided there was a sarcastic tone throughout and that the literary agent was damning him with quaint praise.

He could visualise Audrey Saunders as she wrote the letter that banished hope from his life yet again. There she was in her hi-tech office with a view of a Wren church. Perhaps a lanky man nearby ready to be impressed. A drink in her hand. A secretary taking down the letter to her dictation with a smirk on her red lips. Everywhere around evidence of success. Pictures of Audrey Saunders addressing a Foyles' Luncheon; Audrey Saunders sharing a joke with Jeffrey Archer; Audrey Saunders on top of the world . . .

The cold got to him. He retreated from the hall into the back room of the terraced house. Placing himself over the electric fire, he read the letter again. Then, very deliberately, he folded it repeatedly until it formed a spill and poked it through the grating of the electric fire. He held it against the angry red coil and after much sparking and spluttering the spill ignited. He pulled it away and lit a cheap cigarette.

Like a steam train, Percy Wordsworth fumed from room to room. He filled the kettle and set it on the stove, but, remembering that the gas had been cut off, he lit the Primus stove and banged the kettle down on that instead. He stood by the telephone and contemplated it, then found himself back in front of the meagre warmth of the electric fire. The octagonal mirror on the wall above it caught his face. His brow was deeply furrowed, his mouth had become a downward-pulled semi-circle. He gazed into the mirror and he pitied himself. His chin began to quiver, suggesting the approach of tears, as the rustling of winter trees presages the approach of rain – or worse.

'That damned woman!' snarled Percy Wordsworth. 'I could have paid the gas bill with the money it took to send in the manuscripts. She doesn't give a twopenny fart for literature. Only interested in what will sell. I'd like to . . .'

But the thought evaporated as he wandered back towards the kitchen, recalling that all the stories he had sent to Audrey Saunders *had* been written to sell. He had not wanted to write what he had written. He had slaved over them, bored and depressed, because he felt they would tap a market. Well, either the market had changed or Audrey Saunders had not the vaguest notion of what *would* sell.

The kettle showed no sign of boiling. He fidgeted in front of it for a long moment. Then he pulled a face at his dingy reflection in the kettle and paced back into the living room. He sat down heavily on the bald, instant-coffee-coloured sofa and yelped as his thigh caught one of its exposed springs. With one hand he rubbed at the pain while the other searched for the telephone, completely covered by the wreckage of the previous Sunday's papers. The sight of them reminded him it was Friday. Yes, he'd fix her. He'd ruin her weekend.

Cradling the telephone on his knees, he dialled Audrey Saunders' number.

'Good afternoon. Audrey Saunders and Company. Can I help you?'

He could see the secretary as she spoke. Bored and obsessed with herself. No time for anyone else. Dead eyes fixed on the main chance.

Putting on an American accent Percy Wordsworth said, 'Hi! This is Jack Zeigen. I'm calling on behalf of Doubleday in New York. I'd like to speak to Ms Saunders.'

There was a pause. Just that. No 'I'll put you through'. Nothing. His picture of the secretary hardened.

'Audrey Saunders speaking.'

He inhaled deeply, and, reverting to his own accent, began, 'Oh, it is, is it? Well, let me tell you, Ms Audrey Saunders, that you have about as much taste as a sewer rat. What makes you think that you have any qualifications to judge writers' work? If *Crime and Punishment* had landed on your desk you would have popped it straight in the bin as "Too depressing". I know your type, Audrey Saunders! You're parasites feeding off the sweat of impoverished writers. You're pimps setting up false demands and then satisfying the trashy tastes of the public – tastes that you have created. Anything for a buck! That's right, isn't it, Audrey Tawdry? All you're looking for is another pre-digested morsel to add to the tasteless soup the so-called Arts Establishment of this country has created and keeps cooking to death on a tepid flame. The Human Condition is just a cliché to people like you, isn't it, Audrey Saunders? You with the Princess Di wardrobe and the place in the country! What do you know?'

He paused.

'Ah, does diddums feel rejected? Poor diddums!' replied Audrey Saunders.

Then there was a click and the line went dead.

'Wait! I haven't finished yet!' He put the receiver down, then threw the telephone at the Sunday papers where it made a soft landing.

'I haven't finished yet!' Percy Wordsworth repeated, and the tone of his voice echoing the hatred he felt surprised him. His livid muse pulled him to the typewriter, slapped his rump, sucked his fingers, and commanded him to get down to it.

When the cleaners of Westminster Abbey opened the great doors and shuffled into the building in the pre-dawn cold, they were surprised and taken aback to find the body of the well-known literary agent, Audrey Saunders, sprawled over the Dylan Thomas Memorial Stone in Poets' Corner.

There were no immediate clues as to the cause of death, but the cleaners all said they would never forget the bewildered expression on the face of the once-handsome woman. This expression was rendered somewhat mawkish by the presence of a black Osmiroid fountain pen, the barrel almost cut in half by frenzied biting, the nib buried deep in the soft palate of the victim.

It emerged during the course of the post-mortem that the pen had been the cause of death, or, more accurately, what the pen had contained.

'Prussic acid unloaded from the pen's reservoir into the victim's mouth. Enough to kill a herd of elephants,' was the verdict of the pathologist. 'By the way – ' he was addressing a rumpled police inspector ' – you shouldn't be smoking in this office. It's a nicotine-free zone.'

'Sorry,' replied Inspector Dyer. He inhaled the smoke from his last drag and then stubbed out the cigarette in a wastepaper bin. 'Just can't give 'em up.'

'Me neither.'

Dyer, wearing the smirk for which he was famous, reached into the pocket of his mackintosh and produced a crumpled bag. He opened it and popped a sherbet lemon into his mouth.

'Sweets'll rot your teeth,' said the pathologist.

Dyer offered the pathologist his open bag.

'Thank you very much. You know I used to think that the teeth of the British mirrored society. I used to think that we *were* what became of our gnashers.'

'But you don't think that now?' asked Inspector Dyer, wondering as he chewed whether he ought to crunch into the sweet or suck it until the boiled part weakened and broke of its own accord, releasing the bitter-sweet sherbet.

'No, not any more. They're much too healthy these days and those that aren't healthy can be made to look as though they are. Now that they're all white, well who can tell what's what any more?' The pathologist gazed absent-mindedly out of the window through which the traffic sound of rush-hour London – insanity successfully masquerading as normality – babbled.

'Well, that's as may be,' Dyer said, 'but about the Audrey Saunders death. It's an open-and-shut case. Maybe a bit of searching through the files, but an open-and-shut case.'

The pathologist nodded. 'I like the bit when you crack open the sweet and the sherbet explodes in your mouth.'

Dyer smirked knowingly, then looked at his watch and said, 'Duty calls.'

He left the pathology department and made his way to his Rover in the underground parking lot of Scotland Yard. He gunned it towards the Embankment en route to Audrey Saunders' literary agency. 'An open and shut case,' he mused as he drove. 'Just a case of searching through her files.'

But in this Inspector Dyer was mistaken.

Audrey Saunders Limited
45 Taylor Square
London WC1

17 October

Percy Wordsworth
43 Scaffold Ridge
Fayers
Suffolk

Dear Percy Wordsworth,

I was immensely cheered to receive your chapter. What a good – and original – idea! I was greatly flattered that I am to have a leading part in your opus, albeit as a corpse. Doubly pleased that my humble rejection letter stimulated your creative juices.

If your novel ever makes it down the birth canal, however, we shall have to change a few names, shan't we? But I must confess to being slightly intrigued. I really do wonder how you're going to extend this very good first chapter into a full-length novel. I mean, isn't it going to be rather easy to find out who did it? Won't Inspector Dyer simply have to look through the records to find a suspect? Won't he plod through the letters to rejected authors until he finds a likely lad? Nevertheless, I ache for more. Nay, I *pant* for more! Do let us in on the dénouement. I'm expecting great things of you!

By the way, thank you so much for the scented envelope in which you enclosed your literary bouquet. I had thought the age of chivalry was dead. Evidently not! Such a gorgeous, hypnotic perfume! As I opened the envelope, I practically swooned away. The perfume carried me straight back to Khan El Khalili in Cairo. I was there on my last holiday. Thank you very much indeed.

Sincerely,
Audrey Saunders

Percy Wordsworth was over the moon. Audrey Saunders had received his chapter and had opened the package with her own fair hands! The book on South American poisons in the permanent reserve of his local Carnegie library had told him that the Ghatama tribe's poison of preference would spread throughout the system in twelve hours. The skin did not need to be broken. The poison merely had to touch the lucky recipient. It was undetectable, but he had been able to make it simply enough after a visit to a garden centre and his local unhealthy-looking health food store. Then he had mixed the poison with the dregs of a ten-year-old bottle of Old Spice he had been bought in his youth, and spread the bitter-sweet vitriol over the manuscript.

Audrey Saunders would die – probably already *had* died – of apparent heart failure. Then what would happen next would either complete his book for him or give him time alone in a nice warm cell, where no one cut off the gas or the lecky, to create.

'Thank you, Audrey, thank you!' he exclaimed, as he slid down the hall wall to the floor. There Percy Wordsworth crouched, a literary lion about to pounce.

Yaohan's Sarong

Yaohan, dressed like a princess in her batik sarong of all the colours on earth, surprised the drivers speeding towards the capital. The sight of her, to them, was as strange as coming upon a cascade of spring blossoms in the road. A hail of green banknotes would have come as less of a surprise. The drivers were besieged by green. Jungle, albeit tamed and manicured, but jungle nonetheless, was an everyday sight, an inevitable part of their ride to work. But Yaohan sweeping the dust from the stubble by the freeway in her splendid batik stopped them short.

Sometimes well-to-do ladies would suddenly pull over on to the hard shoulder, almost causing accidents, and beep at Yaohan, offering to buy the batik from her. Yaohan did not understand the harsh foreign syllables but knew exactly why they spoke to her. Politely she smiled and shook her head. She did not mind the women asking her. It made for incident in her day. But the batik was not for sale.

The well-to-do women would start up their cars and roar away from the object of their lust, all the colours of the earth dazzling and retreating from them in their driving mirrors. They would find themselves arriving home frustrated – then shouting at the servants.

Yaohan emptied her municipal dustpan into the bin on the grass verge. Out of habit she looked into the bin to see if the rich had discarded anything that she might be able to put to use, but she found only soft drinks cans. Had she been at home she would have thanked the spirits for her luck and gathered them up. Her brother, Mulwam, could have made them into little lamps and sold them in the market. But here people would have laughed at you if you had tried to sell such a thing. The cans were left to return to the earth. Perhaps the Ancestors had some use for them.

She returned to her brushing and attempted to empty her mind as she had just emptied the dust from the dustpan. It was necessary for Yaohan so to do, for, if she did not, she would think how hot she was, how poor, how far from home, how unfortunate, how dumb in a foreign country.

The Street Cleaning Executive had mimed her to extra efforts that morning. Leaning out of the window of his Landcruiser he had pointed to the flags being erected along the street and then mimed sweeping behind a brush. Yaohan nodded and smiled, though she hated the Street Cleaning Executive. He had taken her off the street one day, driven her to a seedy discarded office surrounded by jungle, and defiled her. He had ripped her sarong. Until he had ripped it she had struggled against him, shouting that she was a street cleaner not a prostitute, but he had not understood her dialect. Roughly he grabbed the corner of her sarong and pulled at it. Yaohan had screamed when she heard the sound of breaking cloth. She backed away from the Street Cleaning Executive and at once removed the garment, placing it lovingly on a dusty desk covered with empty beer cans. The pain of defilement was as nothing when compared to the pain of knowing that her batik sarong had been ripped.

Yaohan knew why flags were being erected. The Sultan who ruled her country was visiting. She brushed but could not blot out of her mind the thought, 'Sultan visiting.' She hated the Sultan with a passion. This Sultan had murdered a fisherman from Yaohan's village. He had been tried for the offence and convicted, but then his father had pardoned him. He had not been a Sultan then. But now he was a Sultan and Yaohan found herself sweeping the streets to impress a murderer, a murderer she would have preferred to see hanging from a gallows she had dusted and polished. But the world was strange. There was no honour or fairness anywhere.

Then, in the rhythm of her sweeping, Yaohan was at last able to dislodge the last specks of dusty thought from her mind. Blankly she brushed away the morning. She barely noticed that each pile of dust she swept was being dispersed in seconds by the speeding wheels of the cars.

At lunchtime Yaohan walked along the central reservation of the road and washed herself at a tap, placed there to keep the grass green. With difficulty, she crossed the road and found her lunch hanging from a branch of a tree. It consisted of cold rice and some fried vegetables. She squatted in the shade afforded by the tree and started to eat. As she ate, ignoring the cars that whizzed by nearby, she allowed herself to think of home. She remembered the day that her mother had suggested it was time to make her wedding batik. They had walked the seven kilometres to the market and bought the required piece of fine cotton cloth. Yaohan's mother insisted on finding the best piece. 'It must be without flaw or stain. It must be like my daughter here.'

The merchant had smiled and produced his finest cloth. He had flirted with her but it had been a small price to pay for the cloth, sold to them cheaply.

With some ceremony Yaohan's mother had presented the piece of cloth to her daughter, telling her to do her best work on it.

'On this cloth you must paint your soul, my dear! Work carefully! Work with love!'

Yaohan had bowed. She did not know with certainty to whom her finished sarong would be presented. She would only know when the recipient returned it with an offer of marriage. But, as she started work on it, searched the jungle around the Kampong for plants that would yield their colours as dye, as she planned out the landscape of her soul, she imagined the face of the Beloved. She had a shrewd idea that Kuanti the fisherman would be the man chosen for her. And she planned the design of her batik to convey the essence of her soul in a way that Kuanti would understand.

She reached down with her right hand to take up a morsel of food, but found that it had all gone. She threw away the banana leaf her small meal had been wrapped in and carefully folded the cloth. She stood and carefully brushed fallen grains of rice from the sarong. She stopped to admire it in the dappled light of the sun percolating down on it through the tree. Ah, but it was beautiful still! The colours were as vibrant as the day they had been applied; repeated washing only seemed to bring them out more strongly.

For a moment she lost herself in a rapt contemplation of her work. She could remember how inspiration had come and what she had been trying to say to Kuanti about her soul. First, she had painted and dyed the green foliage of a banyan tree. The tree had shaded the Buddha while he sought enlightenment. It covered the whole of the cloth. She would shade Kuanti as the banyan had the Buddha. Then Yaohan had plotted the course of a river from left to right across the cloth. The river threaded its way through the branches of the tree, seeming to wrap it in a ribbon. This, Yaohan had decided, would be the course of her life. Presiding over all was a huge orange sun with brown calm eyes and a smile of enlightenment. The sun shone down on the tree and the river, its rays waxed in yellows and golds made from saffron.

Yaohan sat back down under the tree, her brush beside her, to take her customary nap.

Above, the sun was at its hottest. It always seemed to her to be a cruel cousin to the sun that shone on her own country. She had noticed the change in it as she crossed the sea on her way to exile. On her way to a new start in a new country. The agent had promised her that. It would be like being reincarnated into a higher existence, the existence of a rich person. She had told him that she could afford to pay only very little for the opportunity of the job in the rich country, and he had smiled and closed the shutters of his shop.

Sleeping, she dreamed the same dream. Kuanti stood in the shallows of the night ocean and beckoned her to take his hand and walk into the water with him. Yaohan held back and he teased her for her timidity. Then, when she still wouldn't come, he walked off into deeper water until he had all but disappeared from her sight. She looked up at the millions of stars, heard the breaking of the straight rollers, and felt a momentary unbearable loneliness. Then:

'Come!' he called her.

'But how shall I find you in this dark?'

'Silly girl!' And he had splashed at the water around him and thrown it over his body. The phosphorescence illuminated his shape then disappeared into the water around him. He repeated the action and she walked out steadily towards his star-spangled body.

'These are the jewels a fisherman gives to his lady,' Kuanti had said.

Yaohan drifted farther into sleep, the sound of the cars like rain falling on the sea near the shore.

'The Sultan is coming! And you sleep!'

Yaohan opened her eyes. It was the Street Cleaning Executive, leaning from his Rangerover and shouting to her over the traffic noise.

She stood and took up her brush. Without acknowledging the presence of the Street Cleaning Executive, she began brushing dust at the side of the road.

'When the Sultan's entourage has passed we shall come for you. We may be late.' And he winked at Yaohan and she knew she would be the last to be dropped and would be taken instead to the office in the jungle.

She nodded to the man and he drove away.

Brushing, she tried to remember her dream but all she could see were the colours of her sarong. Those colours had figured in her dream, she knew. But the story was lost – as lost as her hope and her youth.

Kuanti had wanted to marry her. That was clear. Had he lived she would have been a fisherman's wife living easily on the shores of an adored ocean that gave them everything they asked for. Their golden children would have played among the nets and gone to the school at the other end of the village which the government had started.

When Kuanti was killed nobody had dared tell her. Partly this was due to the manner of his death; partly to the fear among the villagers that the imparter of bad news is some-how to blame. She had only found out about her lover's death when she saw a sad procession of men walking along the beach. One held a spade, two others carried the body on a plank. They were Kuanti's friends. It was not an uncommon sight. It happened as regularly as the village festivals or the coming of high winds from the east, but Yaohan knew exactly who had died. She had run straight home, locked herself in her room and worked on the batik that told the story of her soul.

News of the manner of Kuanti's death and of its perpetrator, filtered through to Yaohan in her seclusion, and inch by inch she told the story in batik.

She was remembering her dream when she heard the child-ren shouting by the side of the road half-a-mile away and motor-cycle sirens blared. Kuanti had been taking her in his arms, carrying her from the sea. She was swooning away with wonder at the feelings his touch awoke in her and her fingers tingled with the anticipation of creation. She knew which berries and barks would be crushed to form the colours that would show her in ecstasy with her lover, leaving the sea.

The motor-cycles flew past her, shooing drivers from the road. The cries of the children grew louder. She heard them and thought of the children she would not have from her love for Kuanti. Their cries became the cries of the late-aborted foetus, of the poor without a voice hungering for a justice that was not in the world, of a virgin raped by a rapacious public cleaning executive, of a girl with hope draining out of her watching the body of her lover taken to the grave, and then, above all that, the groans of a hag in a ragged, colour-gone batik sarong sweeping dust in an alien street – endlessly sweeping the same dust, day after day, year after year.

Suddenly Yaohan was screaming louder than the children. She dropped her brush and stood waiting as a sleek black car headed slowly down the road. Still screaming she ran out into the road ripping the sarong from her body as she did so. Her screams were joined by the screams of the car's brakes. The driver, as he pushed on the brake, saw for a split-second, like a resplendent spirit clothed in all the colours of earth, the batik sarong swept up into the air, turning, swathing itself in panic above the scene, while the grand gold angel on the front of the bonnet caught Yaohan squarely in the chest and carried her momentarily with it, until, like a pinioned fish she wriggled free and was taken under the tyres. The sarong drifted down gently over the now-still car and landed squarely and flat against the windscreen.

A group of uniformed officials gathered. The door was opened and apologetic faces bent low to reassure the Sultan that everything was being taken care of.

But the brigadier who tried to reassure the startled Sultan did not get any response. The Sultan, eyes aghast, medals shaking on his chest, was staring straight ahead of him into the windshield which framed Yaohan's work of art and showed him himself, standing under the shade of a banyan tree aiming his revolver at a handsome fisherman who was gazing, at the moment of his death, at a beautiful young girl holding out her hands to him from the branches of the tree.

Travel is the Greatest Freedom

Mr Drury had spent a fortnight in New York City researching in the Public Library on 42nd Street. It had, he judged, been time well spent: he had compiled enough material to enable him to go back home to his tiny cottage in Derbyshire and start writing his new book, to be called *The American Soul – A Continent of Islands*.

But now, on the last morning of his time in New York, Mr Drury chided himself for not having explored the city. 'Too late now,' he mused as the taxi took him down to Greenwich Village en route to his last errand.

Now that it was far too late to do so, Mr Drury allowed himself the luxury of wishing he could walk those streets at leisure instead of seeing them only as a blur through the taxi's grubby window. But Mr Drury told his wayward wild side there was only time to collect the huge pile of books he had bought at the Aardvark Bookstore and post them off to himself in England. After that he would have to return to the hotel to pack and then head out for the airport. There would be other times. He had come to New York on serious business, after all.

The man in the John Lennon spectacles at the Aardvark Bookstore handed Mr Drury twelve parcels of books. As he did so he smiled a smile which split his face wide open and said, 'Now you just take these little beauties to the post office. Tell the good people there that you want to send them by the Preferential Budget Book Rate. Should they raise an eyebrow, point out that they've been packed in parcels of no more than nine pounds each and have been bound with post-office-preferred fibrous sticky tape. They will supply you with a canvas bag to put all the parcels in.'

'Yes. Yes. Thank you. Thank you,' said Mr Drury, fumbling the parcels into plastic bags.

'We aim to please, sir,' continued the man. 'Ms Zimmerwoman in her cellar has laboured hard and long over those little parcels. Do not let her down. Remember: it's the Preferential Budget Book Rate you're after. Leaving the Big Apple this very day, you say?'

'Yes, I am, more's the pity. Now let me see,' mused Mr Drury, 'I've got to ask the post office about the er . . . ?'

'The Preferential Budget Book Rate.'

'Ah, yes.'

Mr Drury made for the door weighed down by four large stretched-to-screaming-point plastic bags.

'And don't let them play dumb,' advised the man. The sun's rays as they beamed down over the Lower East Side caught his spectacle lenses and threw back a blinding light at Mr Drury.

'Play dumb? No, I shan't. No, of course not,' he promised.

'Have a good day!'

'Ah, yes. A good day. You too. Cheerio.'

What seemed to him to be an age later, Mr Drury struggled through the double doors of the US post office on 2nd Avenue and 12th Street. With a great exhalation of breath he laid down his bags of books on the dirty marble floor and started to kick them towards the back of the central queue. As he did this he stepped on a hot dog sausage, apologised to it and heard a loud voice echoing through the post office:

'Your money or your life! Your money or your life! Godammit!'

He saw an unkempt, unsteady man at the counter, holding

up a female postal official, using an empty hot dog roll as his weapon.

The female postal official, who looked like Ella Fitzgerald in a bus conductor's uniform, also seemed to sense that the weapon was unloaded. She did not look up from her big book of stamps, but turned over the pages at amazing speed, as if she was dying to see how the story would end. While thus engaged she gestured towards the end of the central queue and boomed, 'Sir! There's a line! Sir! Take your turn!'

The unkempt, unsteady man then turned his weapon on himself and commenced eating the hot dog roll. He chewed at it uncertainly as he walked towards the back of the central queue. When he saw Mr Drury his eyes lit up. He opened his arms wide and commenced a little dance which provided him with the momentum to perambulate himself rhythmically towards him, shouting, 'Hey, man! It's you! Hey, man!'

Mr Drury did not think it was 'him'. Indeed, he prayed that he was not 'him'. A woman in front of him in the queue had turned around and was giving him a look which said that, in her opinion, he was definitely 'him'. Then she said to the rest of the queue, referring, Mr Drury devoutly hoped, not to Mr Drury, 'Drugs! He's drugged out of his mind.'

The drugged man shook Mr Drury by the hand.

'I – er – well – umm,' said Mr Drury. 'I am sure I am not the person you er . . . want.' He hoped he sounded Dumb and Innocent and English and Abroad and Out of his Depth.

The drugged man stopped shaking his hand and asked, 'You English?'

'Well actually, er, yes I am.'

But the drugged man was unconvinced, 'Naar, you're too old to be English,' he said.

Before Mr Drury could absorb the implications of this remark, the woman further up the queue looked at Mr Drury angrily, 'Don't encourage him,' she commanded.

'I wasn't! He just came up to me and . . .'

But luckily the drugged man had swayed away. He ended up resting his head on a customer writing shelf below a sign which proclaimed: TRAVEL IS THE GREATEST FREEDOM.

Mr Drury used the time of waiting to look around him. There were about twelve people in the queue in front of him and an ever growing number behind. All held letters. All looked around them unhappily, centring their attention on the two postal officials who handled the customers. Mr Drury worried about which postal official he would get. He hoped it would be Ella Fitzgerald as he did not like the look of the other official, who seemed to be reducing all his customers to tears of frustration.

'Next!'

Before he knew it Mr Drury was at the front of the queue. He had passed the time listening to the rumblings of discontent behind him. The complaints centred on the paucity of officials catering to the public. When bored by this he watched the drugged man, who, quite soon, had tired of leaning on the writing shelf and was trying to sell anyone who came near a black wallet. Nobody was buying.

'Next!'

'Hey, bud. That means you.' It was the voice of the man who had complained most.

'Me? Oh, yes. Sorry,' smiled Mr Drury and he started carrying his bags of books towards the forbidding postal official.

'Yeah?' asked the postal official. He was overweight, unshaven and seemed extremely unhappy to be where fate had placed him.

Mr Drury gulped and stuttered out his request for the Preferential Budget Book Rate.

'So?' asked the postal official, staring at the sky in the windows behind Mr Drury. 'So?' he repeated inserting the index finger of his left hand into his right nostril and rotating it in an anti-clockwise direction.

'So, I would like to send these parcels please,' said Mr Drury, placing one of the neat parcels, the sterling work of Ms Zimmerwoman, on the counter and frowning at the postal official's nostril.

The postal official did not perceive the full import of Mr Drury's frown, for just at that moment the man who had complained shouted, 'Don't tell me she's taking a break with all these people waiting! Sheesh!'

Mr Drury's postal official leaned over the counter towards the man who had complained. In so doing he dislodged the parcel. It fell to the floor. Mr Drury said, 'Sorry!' and bent down to pick it up. He was beaten to the parcel, however, by the drugged man, who asked him if he'd like to buy the wallet for five dollars. 'Shhh!' said Mr Drury.

The drugged man and Mr Drury looked up to hear the postal official shout, 'Hey, you! You wanna make trouble! She's entitled to her break same as anyone else.'

Then he sat down again and said to Mr Drury and the drugged man, 'Troublemakers make trouble.'

Both nodded at the truth of that. Then the drugged man fled. This would have been a great relief for Mr Drury except that he had fled with one of his parcels of books on his head.

'You,' said the postal official.

'I want to send these books, and the books on that gentleman's head, to England in their own bag please,' announced Mr Drury.

'Give!' commanded the postal official clicking his fingers as he did so. Obediently Mr Drury heaved the parcels on to the counter where, if parcels could quake, they would have quaked before the look of intense distaste directed at them by the postal official.

'Is that all?' he asked.

'No, I'm afraid not. That chap over there has a further parcel of mine on his head.'

'So get it.'

Obediently, Mr Drury made off across the post office to retrieve his parcel. He went up to the drugged man who was whistling 'If I Had a Hammer' rather breathily, while still balancing the parcel of books on his head.

'Please may I have my parcel back, please?' pleaded Mr Drury.

'Buy my wallet. Please buy it. Only five dollars.'

'But I've already got a wallet!' protested Mr Drury.

'Not this wallet you haven't. No, sir! Look it says nine ninety-five on the label. It's from Macy's.'

Mr Drury thought he knew how the drugged man had got it too, but said nothing. The two stood staring at one another for a long moment. Then help arrived in the shape of an elderly black man at the back of the queue, who stepped between them and grabbed the parcel from the drugged man's head, presenting it to Mr Drury as if it were the keys to the city of New York.

'That's no way to treat a visitor,' the black man said to the drugged man.

'Thank you very much. Very grateful,' said Mr Drury.

'Think nothing of it. The name's Richard Earl Brown, sir. I was stationed in Bent Waters Base in Suffolk during the War. You don't happen to know Lilian Fayers at the Live and Let Live public house in Aldeburgh, do you?'

'No. I'm sorry, I don't. I've never been to Suffolk, in fact.'

The black man looked momentarily crestfallen. 'Probably dead,' he said, and with a sad little wave returned to his place in the queue.

Mr Drury trotted back to the counter, where the postal official set about weighing the parcels. Then he disappeared into the back room of the post office muttering, 'Its own canvas bag . . .' leaving Mr Drury with time to watch the unfortunate developments in the queue.

It was not a pretty sight. Twenty or so very angry New

Yorkers were sending looks of complete hatred at Ella
Fitzgerald taking her break. She had chosen not to leave her
station, and was taking tiny sips from a mug which bore the
inscription: I'M THE BOSS AROUND HERE! Between sips she was
counting money and placing sheets of stamps in the correct
pages of her big book. She smiled sweetly as she did these
little jobs. Her smile reminded Mr Drury of a child furnishing
a doll's house; finding a place for everything and smiling a
private smile for the joy of neatness and order brought to
small things. However, it did strike him as somewhat strange
that the postal official could smile so readily while in front of
her a queue of angry New Yorkers stretched, all desirous of
her death.

Mr Drury looked round further. The drugged man was
now sitting on the floor under the notice which read: IDEAS?
COMPLIMENTS? COMPLAINTS? WRITE THEM HERE! Somebody
had written unflattering things about the post office in the
space provided.

'Every day! Every day it's the same!' fumed the man who
had complained, loudly enough for Ella Fitzgerald to hear.
But if she heard, she did not respond. She was now cheer-
fully emptying the water out of her sponge. She squeezed the
sponge tightly between thumb and forefinger and drops of
sticky grey water fell back into the bowl which the suffering
sponge no doubt regarded as home. Then she placed the
sponge back into its bowl and patted it twice affectionately.
At last, she removed the 'Closed' sign from her station and
dropped her smile:

'Next!' she bellowed.

Mr Drury noted that the man who had complained was
next and had gone a funny colour.

Soon after, Mr Drury's postal official returned with a
canvas bag of great antiquity. Into this he pushed the parcels
saying, 'Now you!' to each of the parcels in turn. 'Write your
address on this,' he told Mr Drury.

Mr Drury did so.

'Your name Floral Cottage, eh?' he asked.

'No, that's the name of my house.'

'That a fact? Mine's called Sweep The Step.'

Mr Drury smiled. The postal official looked at him. 'You foreign?' he asked.

'Well, yes. English actually.'

'My Fair Lady,' said the postal official.

'Yes, that sort of thing.'

'Twenty-two dollars and seventy-five cents.'

Mr Drury handed over the money and took his change without counting it.

'Have a good day!' he said to the postal official, a feeling of relief, which, in his confused state, he mistook for warmth towards the man as it welled up in him from sources he did not know he had and which he wondered if he should see a doctor about.

'Have a good day yourself. Next!' replied the postal official.

Mr Drury walked out of the post office, smiling serenely at the queue and determined to walk back to his hotel through the crazy, blessed and beautiful streets of New York City – even though, by so doing, he might lay himself open to embarrassing moments caused by the drugged man, who had followed him out of the post office and was now brandishing the Macy's wallet in his face, intoning, 'Please buy it! Please! Only five dollars! Buy it! Please! It's a goddam steal! Buy it!'

Two months later, back at Floral Cottage, Mr Drury was still awaiting the arrival of his books. His efforts at writing *The American Soul – A Continent of Islands* had come to nothing. His research material lay gathering dust in a corner of his study. He mooned around the house listening to the radio and trying to understand how half an hour in a post office could have so unhinged him.

Still, the trip had not been a complete waste of time. His new wallet had received many compliments. He reckoned he had gotten quite a bargain there.

The Automatic Door-Closer

It was all very sudden. Patrick Wharton woke up one morning in February and found that he was looking down on his death-bed from above.

At first he thought he was dreaming; then that it was somebody else lying in the bed. He even found himself feeling great sympathy for the poor man lying below him – a man not unlike himself – with tubes leading from him, a nurse taking his pulse. A reproduction of Constable's *Hay Wain* hung on the wall opposite. The man had his eyes open and was regarding the painting with some distaste. Poor bugger, thought Patrick Wharton. Then Patrick Wharton slipped off the ceiling and was suddenly that poor bugger, thinking, that damned picture. It follows me everywhere. Even into hospital.

Then the truth of his situation hit him.

He jerked in the bed and the nurse turned towards him anxiously, worried that something beyond her competence was happening. He felt the nurse's hand on his forehead, saw her dark young face for a moment through wide eyes, then closed those eyes abruptly, seeing then, behind his lids, the kindly face of the nurse, surrounded by an aura of light and pin-pricks of falling stars in primary colours emphasised by the surrounding blackness.

The door to his room opened, shut slowly with the sigh made by automatic door-closers. He thought about door-closers waiting behind every door like a one-armed bandit. Then he thought about one-armed bandits, another item of the material world he had never given much thought to. Then he was back to door-closers. How did they work? Who had invented them? Had the inventor retired rich and died a happy and fulfilled man or had he been cheated of his patent by some robber baron to die in penury? And, if the inventor of automatic door-closers had indeed retired, why had he retired before he had ironed out the problem of the sigh? How much irritation, even sorrow, that sigh must have caused! It was beginning to make Patrick want to cry. He heard the nurse running down the corridor, could imagine the sight of her stockinged legs in danger of being tripped by the gingham skirt. Running flesh against material. Voices from the office and two people dashing back towards his room. *Get Doctor Sullivan!* Patrick Wharton opened his eyes, saw the *Hay Wain*, closed them again, little knowing then that his eyes had taken their last look. Too busy telling himself that his turn had perhaps not come.

After all, he thought, as the nurses wiped away the blood from his mouth, it's amazing what they can do these days. Joan in the newsagents had said that just the other day, referring to one of her customers whose *Daily Mirror*s had built up on the hall rug until they had read *Something's Wrong* through the confusing glass of the door and the newspaper boy had told Joan his worries and the police had broken in to find the not-so-old lady in a comatose state in front of 'Breakfast Time'. Joan had been wrong in that case. The woman had died owing two weeks. It was amazing how much money Joan lost from people just dying on her. It was one of the risks of the business.

And if I am to die, what will Joan say when she hears the news? Perhaps Heather from the flat upstairs will tell her when she goes in for her ciggies. Will Joan lean against the till drawer, exhale *He hasn't, has he?* then add, *Did I take for the Kit-Kat? Poor bugger. He was in here – when was it, Abdul Karim lovey? – last week. Done up in his cycling togs. Those new lurex leggings in black. Tell you the truth they didn't do anything for him. Well, you've*

got to have the figure. When am I off? Next Tuesday, God Willing.
We're flying Virgin Upper Class. Miami. Christ, I could do with a
break from this place. Dead, is he? Well it just goes to show. Near
Orlando but not too near . . .

He was aware of the doctor, tried – not knowing – to open his
eyes to see the doctor, to move his lips to say, 'Thank you,
doctor,' when the doctor felt him with his cold hands. But his
eyes would not function and his polite phrase came out as a
whimper. No, he decided. I won't talk again if that's how it
sounds. I must just stay calm and see, well feel, what happens.
It's amazing what they can do. It's amazing really what they can
do. It is really amazing what they can do. No can do. Strange
expression that. Probably Yank.

'I don't think there's much more we can do,' said the doctor.

'No,' replied the nurse.

'Perhaps add ten milligrammes to the morphine solution.'

'Right you are, Doctor.'

Right you are, Doctor! thought Patrick Wharton. Is that it? Is
that the extent of the expertise of modern medicine? Must there
no more be done? I'll write to my MP 'I did not wish to die, Mr
Bleddfa-Buck, but apparently I, as a poor NHS patient, do not
have anything to say in the matter. Bump up the morphine and
bump off the poor bugger. It isn't good enough. And I shall not
vote for you in the next election. Accept a proxy-plague on both
your Houses.' Patrick laughed inwardly. Then he was serious as
the situation became clear again and the door-closer sighed.

It isn't good enough. I am not good enough. To die. I am not
ready. To die. So much left to do and achieve and amend. I am
not ready and I think it a pretty poor show.

Somewhere to his left two nurses were fiddling with something. He heard a sound like an electric razor starting, stopping,
starting again.

'Make sure the clamp fits snugly over the syringe,' said one of
the nurses, 'otherwise the patient doesn't get the full dose at the
right intervals.'

'They're temperamental and that's a fact,' said her companion. 'When do you get off?'

'Seven.'

'Going to the Rose?'

'Ben's taking me to his mum's for dinner.'

'It sounds serious.'

The other nurse did not reply and Patrick was left wondering whether her affair with Ben was serious or not. Still, Ben's a good solid name. Much better than Bill. Roughly on a par with Tom, but Ben's a bit more of a novelty. He tried again to open his eyes but nothing happened. He badly wanted to know, and the realisation that he would not, in all probability, ever learn the end of the story of the nurse and Ben filled him with sadness. What was the nurse's name? He did not even know that. Not to know the name of my angel. And not for the first time either.

The door opened and the sister told the nurses to stop gossiping. Did they not know that hearing was the last faculty to go. They must exercise sensitivity around the patient. He might be able to hear everything and had the relatives been informed. Was he C of E, Catholic, Something Exotic or Don't Know?

Well, Patrick thought. That wasn't very sensitive. She's just told me everything that I would rather not know. I can hear. Is that it? He thought of a large ear lying in bed, the sheet drawn up as far as the half-moon top. The joke when he had heard it and cracked it – at school? In the staff room? A cruel joke from the distant past. *That's not my baby! That's not my baby! It is, I'm afraid. And I have some bad news for you. He's deaf.*

'That's cruel,' Mary, who was never cruel, had said. And Patrick had felt guilty, had looked round to see – to see! – if Mary was around before repeating it in future. But repeat it he had. *Have you heard this one? There was this woman and she had a baby but her baby was only an ear and* . . . And, he thought now as the morphine pump whirred, that's not the best part. The best part is that now *I* am only an ear. If I could laugh, now might be the time. Do I want to go out with a laugh? How do I want to go? Do people go as if acting a part in a weepy? The death bed as star vehicle. Shall I go as my audience wishes? Shall I surprise them? Shall I go out in my own way? But then, trying to open his stuck eyes, reminded, furious for needing to be reminded, I have already gone. It's over but it isn't finished. It is as plain as the ear on your face that I am dying. I never thought it would come to this. Of course, in some part of me I knew it would but I didn't know it would. I knew and didn't know all at the same time. Just as I believed and didn't believe.

Well, here I am. Am I about to make a death bed conversion? Hail Mary full of grace. She was too. Full of it. Like an overfilled pint pot, Mary's grace flowed down her like foam. God, I could do with a pint. Dad was given a Mackeson every night in hospital. He drank his last one down, placed it neatly on the bedside table, said, 'That was just the job. Just the job that', and fell back dead just as I was popping in a grape from the bedside table. He caved in and I cracked the grape. Its cud was still in my mouth when I was signing the forms. I said to everyone, 'It was as easy as falling off a log. He went just like that. I hope it's as easy for me.' It ought to be. I did the Nine First Fridays. Some time ago, I'll admit, but I did them. But maybe this is the chance now. At this very moment. To recant. To relent. Oh my God because Thou art so good I am very sorry that I have sinned against Thee and by the help of Thy Grace I will not sin again. Not that I'm going to get the chance. Question is, would I if I could. Well, that depends on the sin, doesn't it? Assuming it is/was a sin. Decisions. Decisions. I'm not fit to make decisions!

He heard footsteps and the sigh of the door-closer. Then nothing more for a too-long moment. Next it'll be a pillow over my head. A bubble of air injected into a vein. Ugly hell gape not! I'll burn my books! Just give me time and I'll . . .

'He looks very peaceful,' said Patrick Wharton's sister.

'He's got a good colour too,' said Patrick's sister's girlfriend, whom Patrick had never liked. 'It's hard to credit that there's no hope.'

'I told him he was a fool to ride round the city on his bike. He was an accident waiting to happen. Biking for him was a sort of political point,' said his sister, her voice breaking.

'I'll burn my bike!' screamed Patrick inwardly.

'He was always making political points. But what's the point, I say.'

'The patient may be able to hear you,' cautioned the nurse.

But he couldn't.

My cycling. Shall I offer up my cycling to The Lord as my one good act? After all I was giving a good example, trying to save the planet in my own small way. I always turned off lights religiously too. And the gas. Christ, did I leave the gas on when I left the house to go to the National and . . . well it must have happened on the way. I'm sure I'd have remembered the play. *After the Fall*. Don't remember a thing about it. The question is, did I leave it on? I was slow cooking an All Bran loaf and I often leave it on in order to return to it piping hot and a little overcooked just as I like it. Well, I don't like it much but I do the following morning. A good three flusher. There's nothing like it.

'Did you see that? Do you think he's trying to tell us something?' asked his sister

'He's past all that now,' said the nurse.

That's the truth, nurse, he thought. It would have been nice to arrive at this moment quite prepared – the gas off, a life of quiet virtue safely stacked away, the paper-bill paid, the homeless – now housed – calling at the hospital and telling the sister how I had offered him and many another my spare bedroom. 'He wouldn't take a penny. I swear to God without Patrick I'd still be on the streets and that's a fact. He gave me a breathing space. If there's a heaven then I know that's where

Patrick is.' Letters coming in from the Hungry I sponsored round the starved world. Yes, it would be nice. Instead I spent my money on weight-on food supplements and compact discs and carbon fibre frames for the bike. When the moment comes I'll just be one more Adam, his nose in the dirt, offering a few scraps of mixed-motive generosity to weigh against a life devoted to ducks on doilies. What will God make of me? Will it be pitchforks and leering red devils for all eternity or will I scrape though like the last fat, chap-legged kid picked for a football team?

'His breathing's very irregular. It can't be long now,' said the nurse.

'It just goes to show,' said Patrick's sister's friend.

'What does that mean, silly cow! Your turn will come!' thought Patrick uncharitably. Then he recited another act of contrition, his second in five minutes. His second in forty years. He heard, very dimly, footsteps and, from a great distance, the sighing as the door closed. He thought of the gas at home, worried about it for a while. Then he remembered the inventor of automatic door-closers. Had he been hauled over the coals for not banishing the sigh? He hoped not and said a prayer for the inventor. After all, without the sigh he would not have known the door was closing, even that there was a door to close. He sighed . . .

Worlds Away

'This evening's performance of *Worlds Away* will commence in the Olivier theatre in five minutes,' said the tannoy.

There was a log-jam as the group of summer school students, led by Lynn, corralled from behind by Rachel, passed through the corridor and got their first sight of the huge theatre, already almost full. Rachel stood at the end of the row and told the snake of English language learners to pass right along to the end. Lynn took the last seat at the far end of the block booking. But then Ezekiel tried to slip into the middle. Rachel held him back. 'I want you next to me. You have a tendency to wander off,' she said. Ezekiel, though he was a headmaster in Niger and a chief of the Songhai tribe, nodded his compliance. When everyone else was seated Rachel let go of his arm. Then she sat down on the last seat, like a cork sealing a bottle.

The stage was bare, its whole surface covered in gravel raked into horizontal and vertical lines. She looked at Ezekiel. He was sitting low in his seat, reading the cast list. Rachel relaxed, patting herself on the back for giving a free ticket to Ezekiel. He was a scholarship student on the summer school but seemed short of spending-money. She had seen him collecting the tiny packets of sugar, salt and mayonnaise from packed lunches provided for the previous Saturday's trip to Brighton. When asked why, Ezekiel had said they were gifts for his pupils at home. She filed the information away.

Ezekiel was busy adding the Olivier to all the other things he would have to tell everyone when he got home. But not

London, not this theatre, could compare with his first ever sight of sea in Brighton. The sea! A rolling wet desert whose dunes slipped over white, crashing into troughs. Ezekiel had shouted to the waves, encouraging them to greater efforts. Standing at the brink he had cupped sea in his hand and swallowed a mouthful. Fish and salt and soap. How would he tell the children in their assembly lines, desert stretching around them in all directions, that there was a land to the north that was surrounded by water and salt and soap? *Everything we need but unusable!* he had told Rachel. She had looked out over the sea but could not see anything in it. When she looked back at Ezekiel, however, his smile made her step back a pace.

The lights went down. The hum of the audience abated. Ezekiel did not think he had ever seen such dark. If he opened his mouth and ate the darkness it would be as gummy as raw dough. He tried to stare through it to see what was happening on the stage. A scream from every loudspeaker made him jump.

'Oh, my God!' he exclaimed.

'Shhh!'

A single beam of light from the stage caught the audience. It fanned back and forth, taking in the whole theatre, section by section. Then it was extinguished; the stage lit up by a bright light that made him blink, that seemed like the desert at home at midday. But the stage was different. In the time between the dimming of the lights and now – how long? Thirty seconds? – a small bungalow had been erected. It had taken the government five years to build his headmaster's prefab. He could see into the main room where a middle-aged woman was sitting at her desk. A fan rotated above her. Electricity too! And all so quick!

'Wonder!' said Ezekiel.

Rachel reached across and squeezed Ezekiel's hand to try and restrain him. He looked at her hand, wondering about it.

A man in his fifties came into the room, wearing the robes of a priest. He talked with the woman for a long time. Ezekiel worried because he could not take in what they were saying, so distracted was he by a group of ragged bandits treading stealthily around the bungalow, pangas and pistols in their hands. He wanted to tell the couple inside the bungalow to watch out. This need seemed to communicate itself to Rachel who touched his hand again. Something terrible was going to happen.

Then the priest took the woman in his arms and they embraced. Ezekiel tried to concentrate. The bandits were getting closer. The man who seemed to be the leader, a cartridge belt swung diagonally across his sweating chest, was staring at the couple through the louvred window leading on to the veranda. Then he and his companions were still.

The woman and the priest were talking again. Should they go or should they stay? Ezekiel wanted to tell them that either way there was no escape for them. The only thing they could do to save their lives was to offer the robbers everything they had. They might be spared. It was hard to tell. It had worked for Nathaniel Palumbo, his head of geography, while on a course in Lagos. The woman started to open the door of the veranda and the bandit had his panga raised in the air, preparing to strike.

'Mrs! Don't!'

'Shhh!'

Rachel's leg pushed against his.

The woman opened the door on to the veranda, looked out over the audience and said, *This is my home. I do not want to be anywhere else.* Rachel wanted to weep for her. In twenty years as a wandering English language teacher she had hoped, but never quite managed, to say that. But now, though she had found no home, neither was England her home. *Where did I go wrong?* The woman's face was exultant. She stepped outside under the hot sun. The sun increased in intensity for a split second, then went out and strobe lights caught the bandit's panga falling, chopping, rising with a lightning glint. As in a silent film, the priest moved behind the woman to protect her, and pangas from the other men came together and fell on him. The bandits disappeared and the couple, caught by a single beam from the back of the theatre, covered in wounds and dripping blood, fell together, but slowly, so slowly, swooning to death in one another's arms. The light went out.

'No!' gasped Ezekiel.

'Shhh!'

'Oh, very terrible!'

Rachel's leg and hand. He shuffled his extremities away, embarrassed.

The stage lit up in a trice to show the leader of the bandits dressed in a suit behind a large glass-topped desk. He was speaking on a white telephone. There were many on the desk. Ezekiel knew such men. He had sat humbly outside the offices of such men, waiting to be admitted to plead for school books, for pencils. Where had the bungalow gone? *Ah, how unreliable prosperity is!* And how had the man managed to get into that suit. He did not seem to be sweating at all now. And where was the blood?

A white man came in and started talking about two missionaries who had been murdered at their mission station some years before. The Pope, the man said, wanted to make the priest a saint. What did the minister think of that?

The minister replied that he had other things on his mind. But as long as the investigators from the Vatican were not intrusive, permission would be given. The two men parted amicably enough, arranging to meet one another for a round of golf at the Club.

Ezekiel nodded happily, for the scene had contained much that he knew but had never talked about. The expatriate minister who had fought for independence by fair means and foul who then, when power was offered, forgot the people he had been fighting for, became a stranger insulated by Mercedes windscreens and shiny suits; who flicked down automatic windows to beat with an ivory-tipped cane the poor who came to sell him simple things from a tray.

Black again. Ezekiel waited for the next miracle. Lights up on an English drawing-room set out on the gravel. Only the room was illuminated, the rest of the stage in doughy dark. A woman entered whom Ezekiel thought he knew, followed by a man. Yes, it was the woman he had seen done to death in the bungalow. What had happened? Had she only been wounded? There did not seem to be any scars.

'But she's dead!' Ezekiel told Rachel.

'We've gone back in time.' Her hand found his again.

'Ahh.'

'Shhh!'

The woman seemed very upset because her father was dying; the doctor did not hold out any hope at all. He left shaking his head. Then an older woman, whom the dead woman called 'mother', came in. She said that her father had passed away. The daughter looked sad. She was weeping but Ezekiel did not see any tears.

'She is not sincere! Ungrateful daughter!'

'Shhh!'

The two women talked for a long time about what the man had meant to them both but, when alone, the daughter looked straight out at the audience, exultant; as though life were about to begin for her. Ezekiel fancied she was looking at him and returned hers with a look of reproach. She did not acknowledge him and he waggled his index finger at her.

'Why isn't she sad?'

'Shhh!'

'Ezekiel,' Rachel said gently, in conflict. 'Please don't make noise during the second half. You're distracting everyone.'

'I am sorry,' Ezekiel replied, hangdog.

She tried to repair relations. 'Would you like an ice-cream? My treat.'

'It's a bit predictable,' said Lynn.

Rachel looked at Ezekiel hard. 'If it is, I don't know what to predict.' She had forgotten about his ice-cream. He would have liked one. The little spoon and the plastic cup, playthings for the youngest.

'Some good effects,' said Lynn.

'Yes, not bad at all. A touch melodramatic,' said Rachel.

The stage was bare and the priest came on. He gave a long sermon about serving the missions and converting the heathen. Then the man from the desk, the murderer, talked at length about his hard life. He had been educated at the mission school. He still half-believed everything he had been taught. But if the Pope in Rome canonised the priest he would know that it was all a lie. Because he knew that the priest was no saint. Ezekiel yawned noisily, not trusting the man at all.

The young woman who had just lost her father came up to the priest on the bare stage. She was rich, she said. But she wanted to earn treasure where no thief could break in. She wanted to be a missionary.

'You should take care of your mother. Then you won't get killed by bandits,' Ezekiel shouted up at her.

'Shhh!'

The priest said that her money would be very useful in the mission fields. What else did she feel she had to contribute? The woman did not answer. She and the priest froze on the stage and Ezekiel sighed audibly. He could not concentrate on the scenes that followed. He had wanted to know what she had to contribute. He really wanted to know, to hear it articulated.

Rachel's hand reached him again. He could not go any farther away. 'Please!' she said. What did she mean? He had not spoken.

The frozen couple went into the dark and another priest was interrogating an old woman. She had been the housekeeper at the mission. She had loved the missionaries. Yes, there had been miracles. A man of the village, blind since birth, had miraculously received sight; a woman wasting away had been restored to health . . .

The action shifted to the other side of the stage. The priest kissed the men Ezekiel recognised as his murderers, now dressed in rags and holding crutches. They threw away their crutches.

'Miracles!' shouted Ezekiel.

'Shhh!'

The stage was aglow with light and the sound of the restored men dancing on the gravel. The light grew in intensity and seemed to concentrate upon the priest in the centre of the stage with the people dancing their joy around him. He lifted his arms up and out to the audience. The light around him became unbearable. Ezekiel made to stand with the exaltation he felt at the sound and light and glory of it. Then all went black except for a single spot on the man, the murderer behind the desk. He watched the canonisation of the priest and then laughed. The laughter took up his whole body. He rocked and the laughter echoed all round the theatre, though it seemed to falter when Ezekiel was heard shouting 'Murderer! Hypocrite!' at him. Then the light slowly faded, along with the laughter.

There was silence, a whoosh of applause. The actors bowed. Ezekiel watched them. They watched him. He looked daggers at the actor who had laughed. He did not clap.

The audience filed out, those around the summer school's block booking little knowing then that with the passing of years they would remember the play hardly at all, but the African they had tried to shut up would keep coming back into memory: in other theatres, watching other plays, bored but stoical or quietly appreciative. *When was it? Can't remember. An African chappie. Completey wrapped up in it. Seemed to believe it!*

No, I agree, the theatre's not what it was. All style and no substance.
Fancy an ice-cream? My treat.
   And Rachel too would remember that night, worlds away.
   Shhh . . .

The Devil and Mrs Fox

Goody, it isn't too crowded today. Have you got a pound coin to emancipate a trolley for us? Don't tell me you haven't. We've come here for a good shop, Mrs Fox. And we can't enjoy a good shop with just a basket as you well know. Look in the bottom of your bag. There's bound to be one there, even though it may have mated with a minto. Yes, it *is* a shame that we have to deposit a pound in order to get a trolley but that's how the world is these days. Remember the one we saw being wheeled by that old duck outside the Building Society? She had everything she owned in that trolley. The smell coming off her! Yes, I agreed with you at the time. Why couldn't she have exercised more self-control in her life? There was just no excuse for allowing her standards to slip in that manner. Poor deceased Mr Fox would have smiled down his ascent – or would he have smiled up his descent? Oh, good. You've found a pound at last. Now we can enter Shangri-La! Ha-ha!

Why don't we try one of those lettuces with the frilly red ends? They're so pretty and they're the exact plum red that you've got on your Spode dinner service. We could invite Mrs Craig down for dinner and serve a salad on those plates, a salad featuring colour-coordinated lettuce. She won't say anything of course. But she'll get the message when she sees the artful arrangement and how everything goes. She'll probably go straight back upstairs and parcel up her old ironstone set for Oxfam. And not before time. Remember the chip on that cup? If we weren't so well brought up we'd have smashed it there and then against her onyx table top. Still, we always put charity first. As you so rightly say, *It's better to do without the hygiene than offend the washer-upper*.

Yes, the red frilly lettuce does cost more than the iceberg but look what you're getting, Mrs Fox. Don't worry, we'll bag the rest of the veg ourselves and not pick up the pre-packaged offerings. Yes, you're right again. *Look after the pennies and the pounds will look after themselves*. I must write that down with all the other wise sayings of yours I've collected over the years. There. I'll never forget that now. A pity that smelly woman with her possessions in a trolley could not have taken that sentiment to heart before it was too late, don't you think? That's one of the nice things about our relationship. You and I, we always agree. And that's important. It's a pity there isn't more of it in the world.

Right. We have all the vegetables we require, I think. Let's be methodical and do an aisle at a time. Coffee. If you want me to be honest – and I know that is another thing you value about our friendship – I think it is time we made the taste-leap past instant. You have that cafetière Avril bought you last Christmas. It's in the display case behind the television looking very attractive, very attractive indeed. But unused, unsung. Possessions need making a fuss of too, you know. Yes, I know, you *do* look at it every day and think of Avril, but is that enough? Keep it for best by all means. Let's splurge on *real* coffee. Don't we owe it to ourselves? Don't we *deserve* it? Mr Fox left us well-provided for. And look, if you buy three of their premium blend you save fifty pence. That's not to be sneezed at, is it? Go on! That's good.

We need tea too. I think bags, don't you? Look around. I'll just wait here and guard the trolley, making sure that no wicked person adds *drain cleaner* to the coffee we've purchased, or sprinkles it on the veg. I know it's unlikely but I would have said it was impossible until a few years ago. Now? Well, now it is another of those things we have learnt to live with. The price of shopping security is eternal vigilance. Keep looking. Don't worry about me. I can also watch the citizenry at prayer – at shop. See how they graze! What a picture!

There isn't much of a queue at the delicatessen. Quick, grab a number before that woman with the brimming trolley. Well done. You're sixty-seven. They're serving sixty-four so it shouldn't be much of a wait. Will you look at the rubbish sixty-eight has got in her trolley! Sixty-eight is obviously buying for a big family but she hasn't read the latest findings on healthy eating, has she? Those catering packs of fish fingers. All those technicolour jellies. Her kids are probably walking time-bombs just waiting to go off. That one hanging on to her coat looks as if he's going off as I speak. All those chemicals coursing through them. I can't detect a single pack of fresh vegetables. It's nothing less than wicked. Those kids of hers will be ringing doorbells and running away, drawing unwholesome things on benches in the park. Still, I know what you think and I agree with you wholeheartedly: it's the teachers who are to blame. Spare the rod. But it's the parents too. Off to the pub. And 'Top of the Pops' can't help.

Our turn! Taramasalata. A good choice if I may say so. That'll impress Mrs Craig. And the pink is an exact match of the tablecloth you so lovingly ironed last night. And *hummus*! Ah, hummus! Dinner is going to be a culinary world cruise I see! But are you sure hummus is a wise choice? It always gives me wind. I think it probably gives Mrs Craig wind too, though she'd never admit it. Still, why not? I don't think much of the woman serving us, do you? Face like a lemon and she's spilt some hummus over the Parma ham. I know what you think, and I agree with you. What possible point is there in working in a supermarket if you can't manage to be nice to the customers? A smile doesn't cost anything. What was it you said about smiles? *Let your lips be like a semi-circle with the ends pointing heavenward.* I tell you, Mrs Fox. You ought to send your little sayings to the papers. Take your purchases. Still not the glimmer of a smile. You give her a prize one back to show her what Christianity means. No, she's still as sour as a Saudi Arabian Sunday. Of course, they probably don't have supermarkets where she comes from. Captain Craig tells some stories! It's enough to make your hair curl.

Now it's time for our chilly cliffside walk above the frozen food cabinets. Wrap your paisley round, tuck it in. Button up your Jaeger. Yes, that Jaeger's given you excellent value. I can still remember the day you trotted off clip-clop to buy it at the January Sales. I stayed behind with Mr Fox. You could be relied upon to make the right choice. You don't want me with you every second, do you? Sometimes it's much better if you are just put on automatic pilot. Anyway, I always liked to stay with Mr Fox, especially when he was tinkering with his car. It was a joy to behold, wasn't it? Sixty-eight thousand miles on the clock and not a mark on her! That was the day the winter winds blew your back door shut and Mr Fox had to beg Mrs Craig's hospitality when evening shadows fell and you showed no signs of returning victorious with your booty. You called him a silly goose . . . *Did* Mr Fox say he had taken shelter at *The Short Sharp Shock* public house? Well, I could have sworn he was at Mrs Craig's. But then I may be mistaken and I don't have your razor-like mind. Well, it doesn't matter. I do remember that you bought him a little rubber wedge from the hardware shop the very next day. We've still got it. It's been a real boon.

A leg of New Zealand lamb? Go on, take two! We can put the other in the freezer. You know what a reassuring feeling you get from having your freezer well-stocked. Let winds blow. Oceans roar. The nine o'clock news makes us morbid for a moment. We only have to meditate on our full freezer, add to this thought the excellent provisions made for us by dear Mr Fox, and we're feeling as right as rain in no time. You'll easily be able to defrost the joint in time for Mrs Craig. A quick zap in the micro, being careful to evacuate the room, of course. One can't be too careful.

We really should attempt to give Mrs Craig an evening to remember. Between you and me, Mrs Craig is not a happy woman. Married to a sailor. It can't be easy. You know what sailors are. You may have noticed those parcels of newspapers she puts out with the rubbish. Now it's not my place to tell tales, but I have reason to believe that those packages conceal empty litre bottles of British Cream Sherry. There are at least three a week. Now it could be that she wraps them up because she fears your disapproval for not taking perfectly re-usable bottles to the bottle bank. We, being as we are extremely ecological in our approach, disapprove of that, while appreciating that it is difficult to trundle bottles a mile-and-a-half if you haven't got a car. But I think it far more likely that Mrs Craig is a secret drinker and fears to be found out. Have you noticed how puffy she appears sometimes? What causes her to do these things? Well, your guess is as good as mine. It could be her wretched marriage. Or it might be guilt, I suppose.

Which wine? That is the question. There's an absolutely amazing range. It seems as if all the grapes of the world have been pressed into service for our befuddlement. Mr Fox always favoured claret, but would that be wise for Mrs Craig? There are a range of low-alcohol wines on the market. Yes, I agree, they don't come cheap. But why not buy a bottle just to try. It might be the saving of Mrs Craig. Pull her back from the brink on which she teeters. If it tastes like drain-cleaner – well we won't have to repeat the mistake, will we? This one says it has the taste and aroma of a fully matured Burgundy. Anyway, nothing's too good for Mrs Craig. She's been a good neighbour to you.

Why guilt, you ask? Well, I always like to set you a little conundrum, Mrs Fox. I'll let you think about it some more as you buy the ingredients for dessert. *Trifle!* I was hoping you'd say that. It's not good for our waistline but it is wickedly divine. Devilishly good. While you collect the cherries, almonds, milk and cream, I'll give you a few hints as to why

Mrs Craig might be feeling guilty. I'm not going to make it too easy for you, though. Mr Fox would have been the first to tell me to make sure I kept you guessing. He was a great believer in sharpening the mind. Remember his Scrabble games? The stuff of legend.

I'll give you a hint. Your week at Avril's. Alone. Pass? Well, I've started so I'll finish. You came back and when you came to do the wash a pair of Mr Fox's boxer-shorts was missing. That was not like Mr Fox. You searched high and low and then forgot about them, even though you had bought them for his birthday. Nothing? Let's go on to *household cleansers*.

We're fine for detergents. Washing-up liquid? It's always nice to have a spare. We could buy the ecological one. But what's the point if everyone isn't doing it? It might look good on the draining board but it costs the earth and there's no excuse for that. No, we'll get the usual. We must show some loyalty in a world of shifting allegiances. Some fidelity.

Nothing? You haven't puzzled it out yet? I'll give you one more hint. And then I'm going to drop the matter. Mrs Craig and the brass door-knocker. Ah, you've got it. Yes. We went up to her flat because the postman had left a parcel with you when Mrs Craig was out. Mrs Craig was busily brassoing her door-knocker using as a cloth . . . Mrs Fox! At this point decorum is called for . . . Don't look like that. What will people think? Using as a cloth Mr Fox's jockey-shorts. They had racing-cars on them. Of course, you thought at the time that it was merely a similar pair. A pair of boxer-shorts which, like Captain Craig was always doing, had slipped its anchorage to sail away into Mrs Craig's duster drawer. But no.

No. As you say, *truth will out*. You're a wise woman, Mrs Fox.

Smile. Yes, smile. Hold on to that. Point the edges of those attractive lips towards heaven. Smiles take years off you. Let's see if we can make Mrs Craig smile tonight. Now is there anything else we need? The Lavblu has stained the aubergine porcelain of the downstairs loo blue. Give it a miss. We really ought to sue. Yes, smile. Ah, you've remembered something. Good. Drain cleaner. Put it over there away from all the carefully chosen comestibles, Mrs Fox. We don't want any nasty accidents, do we? Yes, smile again like that. I love to see you smile. All our efforts today will surely make Mrs Craig smile too. And smiles takes years off you.

The Sentence

Niakas, the supreme man of the Kas people, did not like the feeling of the shirt against his shoulders. He did not like the feeling of the shirt on his back or torso either, but, on his shoulders, the material irritated the part of his pendulous earlobes where they touched the grey cotton cloth. Indeed, the parts of his cord-like lobes which emerged front and back from the heavy ear-stones had turned livid and red in just a few hours of periodic contact with the shirt. By the time he reached the place of the men-who-open-the-sky, the tree fellers, Niakas knew that the delicate cord of his lobes would be bleeding. Flies would come to feed and infect the place. And there were no women to find and chew the leaves and smear on the salve that would bring relief.

Walking with four of his men under the canopy of the rainforest, Niakas looked up at the green and knew that he had come farther from his home than most of his tribe had ever been. Only the man-who-speaks-to-the-canopy had been farther and had given him the shirt to wear. The high trees he recognised as those that grew over the home of the Kas, but the patterns of sky behind the canopy were different, foreign, and formed no picture in his head. In Niakas' part of the forest, every inch of the canopy was known and had its own pictures and its own meaning. The canopy between his people and the hot sky and the cruel spirits above was the first thing a Kas child saw upon being born.

Mothers lying in childbirth took comfort from the sight of the canopy and were told by the midwives to see the kindly faces of the Shade Spirits in the million green-and-sunbeam leaves. It was easy for the writhing women to do this for they had been shown how to find the smiling faces of the Shade Spirits from the days of their own births, when, placed on the ground, still covered in the sweet home-smelling juices of birth, they had been given their first lesson in the religion of the Kas, left there naked to pleasure the spirits and told to look for the faces of their Protectors in the canopy high above their heads. The newborn babies cried at first. They could not see what they had to see. Mother and midwives chanted to the spirits of the canopy, pleading with them to show themselves to the new baby. For only when they ceased weeping and looked up-wards did the tribe consider that a new member of the Kas had been born. Then and only then could the celebrations begin.

Niakas, in his grey cotton shirt, led the four men along the track. Nobody spoke. But Niakas could hear the thoughts of his companions. He knew that they were full of fear and he repeated to himself the sentence that Tokas – the man-who-hears-the-canopy, Tokas, who had travelled away from the tribe for many years – had seen where the Kas river married the ocean, had lived in the great City, and who had then returned to the Kas a wise man full of tales – had told him to say to the men-who-open-the-forest. He knew the words by heart. He would not forget the words in all his life, but he repeated them to himself as he walked so that the men behind would not understand his own fear. It was important that his fear, his terror, remain hidden from them. The four were the bravest men of the Kas, but even the bravest men could fail when forced to travel out of the land of the canopy and into the realm of the cruel gods of the sky and the burning fire.

The man-who-speaks-to-the-canopy had sat at the base of the tree which the Kas call Father for seven days and seven nights before calling Niakas to him and whispering the sen-tence. Throughout that time he had fasted. Only when rain fell from the leaves above him, had he lifted his head, his toothless mouth agape, to receive the drops – as if those drops were messages from the spirits of the canopy. It only rained when the cruel spirits of the sky were sleeping and had drawn a covering of cloud about them. Then the gods of the canopy took charge and could be heard by the Kas.

The message was whispered into Niakas' right ear, while the man-who-speaks-to-the-canopy held on to his ear-lobe, putting his thumb and forefinger round the lobe like another ring or like a link in a chain. Niakas held himself very still, for to move might mean the tearing of the lobe. It was considered a great insult by the Kas to even touch the distended looped rope of the ear. For if it were to be broken – and the distended lobe was a fragile thing – then it was thought that the wisdom of years would be broken too; that a man would become a child again. Worse than a child. Not all the salves of the forest could restore the lobe once ripped. It was indicative of the respect accorded to the man-who-speaks-to-the-canopy that Niakas should make himself so vulnerable.

Niakas had smelt the old man's fetid breath as he repeated the message five times into Niakas' ear. Niakas did not move until he felt the lobe released, and even then he had delayed, waited respectfully, the lobe moving like a pendulum and brushing the shoulder of the man-who-speaks-to-the-canopy.

'Go now!' the old man had said. 'Go and tell them.'

Niakas had stood up straight and looked up into the canopy of the forest above their heads, that canopy which for a week had been the man-who-speaks-to-the-canopy's inspiration. And as he looked he saw a woman's face made of distant leaves and branches. Then he looked down at the old man. 'I shall tell them what you have said.'

'The land of the Kas ends just down the road – at the confluence of the Rivers Kas and Tenom,' said the Dutchman to his companion in the Landrover.

'Bleak bloody spot,' remarked his companion, an Englishman, aiming a miserable expression at the landscape of torn trees, powdery soil and yellow earth-movers through which they were driving.

'You just wait,' said the Dutchman, trying to encourage the Englishman and make him think of something other than his churning bowels and livid mosquito bites.

But then the Landrover turned a sharp bend in the track and chugged up a small hill. The two men found themselves looking down at two blue forks where the Kas and Tenom rivers joined. On the near side a yellow and grey logging camp, but, if one ignored that, it seemed as if the earth was a green ocean. In coming over the hillock, all the desolation that had accompanied them from the coast was left behind and a new world took over.

'Do you think there'll be trouble?' asked the Dutchman.

'I hope not, but you never can tell,' the Englishman replied. 'God, it seems to be getting cooler already. I can breathe again.'

The Dutchman nodded. 'The effect of the forest,' he said.

The Landrover drew up outside some cabins. The Dutchman got out and his attention was drawn to the ground, where a black dog lay, prone in sleep, its dugs in the dust. The sight reminded him of Romulus and Remus, but he wondered what their equivalent here were going to build. When he looked up the door of the cabin was filled by a large man in a hard hat. The Dutchman smiled at the man but his smile was not returned and he feared the worst.

'Hello. Van Drimmelen from UPI. This is my colleague Mr Walker.' Van Drimmelen held out his hand but the man did not take it.

'You have taken the wrong road. There is no story here,' he said.

'Ah, everywhere there is a story,' replied Van Drimmelen.

'Go back the way you came,' said the man. 'This is private property.'

'This is the land of the Kas, I think. Are you Kas?' asked Van Drimmelen.

There was a shout from inside the hut. The man at the door took a step towards Van Drimmelen, who automatically held out his hand again. This was ignored and a uniformed man with impenetrable sunglasses on his face and an army uniform took the other man's place.

'You heard what he said. Hit the road!'

'Pleased to meet you,' said Van Drimmelen, the hand that had been held out to shake the hand of the other man, still held out serving, he thought, for the army officer. 'Might I ask you a few questions?'

'I said, hit the road! Pronto!'

Van Drimmelen smiled at the Army man and wondered where he had acquired his quaint expressions.

'We want to know if you plan to take your logging into the land of the Kas?' he asked, still smiling.

The army officer did not reply. He had just got up from watching an episode of 'Dynasty' on a video. A man not unlike this Dutchman in appearance had been wheeling and dealing in a room furnished with hardwood. All white people lived like that. The army man wanted to live like that too, and the forest would help him towards that goal. The Japanese wanted the wood of the Kas and their Chinese agents were prepared to pay him well.

'What do you know?' asked the army man, thinking of his wife and family in a crumbling government block in the city where the electricity failed and where his family could hear everything that was going on above, below and on both sides of them.

'I know that if you destroy the rainforest you will cause the earth's lungs to collapse. I know that.'

The army man did not reply at once. He smiled ruefully and thought, And when you were stomping on us and taking from us everything that we valued, did we lecture you? Would we

have survived to reach your queen and say, 'They are destroy-
ing our heritage! They are offending our traditions!' No, we
will not listen to you. I know you. But all he said was, 'Last
chance! Hit the road!'

'Believe me, your country will become a wasteland if you
continue.'

The army man took out his gun and fired into the air. From
all sides soldiers came. They surrounded Van Drimmelen and
Walker and led them away, locking them in a hut.

The army man smiled and looked past the row of earth-
movers to the half-completed pontoon bridge across the Kas.
In two or three days the bridge would be completed and the
earth-movers would be in the land of the Kas, taking great
tree-full bites from the Kas earth and sending the timber
screaming down the rivers to Japanese workshops. The
Chinese agent would slip him a roll of bills and he would turn
his back and free his family from the stifling flat in the city.

Niakas heard the gunfire. He stopped and, in stopping, lost
the sentence from the man-who-speaks-to-the-canopy. He
thought about the meaning of the shot but then soon forgot it
in his anxiety to once again remember the sentence he had to
communicate. He stood stock-still. A hornbill flew overhead.
A monkey called somewhere to their right. Niakas felt lost and
hopeless for a moment, but then the sentence came back to
him and, the gunfire forgotten, he continued on towards the
confluence of the two rivers.

The army man saw Niakas and his companions standing on
the far side of the river. Fear made him shiver. But it was not
fear of warriors with blow-pipes and distended ear-lobes, but a
fearful recognition that there stood himself but for the lucky
chance of an army-recruitment poster. How such men were
laughed at in the city! Those who had fled from the canopy to
the city lived in squalor. Whenever he saw them he was

reminded uncomfortably of his roots. He felt his tight little ear-lobes and thought of the plastic surgeon.

He watched, and his soldiers watched, as Niakas and his companions forded the river. They walked up to him, their skins gleaming gold in the wetness from their wade. This wetness reflected the light of the falling sun. Niakas, still wearing his shirt, led the way.

The army man looked towards his soldiers and noted that they were smiling, but knew that their smiles concealed fear. He called to one of them who spoke the Kas language.

'Ask them what they want,' he commanded the man.

The soldier, still smiling, stepped up to the naked tribesmen, swaggering, his rifle placed jauntily over one arm. He spoke, and then turned to the army man.

'He says they have travelled far,' said the soldier.

'Their travel is no concern of ours. What do they want?'

'What do you want?' asked the soldier.

Niakas barely understood the soldier. The scene in front of him had banished his pride and his confidence. The officer stood above him with his black eyes that told him nothing of his soul. The soldiers smiled and giggled. He looked at his companions and noted that one had placed his hand in front of his groin to conceal himself. He wanted to do the same, but refrained.

'What do you want?' repeated the soldier, louder.

Niakas wanted to tell the men that he had come to ask them not to invade the land of the Kas. He had poetry in his head that he could recite which would surely melt their hearts and turn aside the yellow machines. He could say all the things in his heart which were a distillation of the things in the hearts of all his people. But his mouth would not work. He could only remember the sentence given him by the man-who-speaks-to-the-canopy.

'What do you want?' shouted the soldier.

Niakas closed his eyes and remembered the sentence once

more. He repeated it one last time to himself. Then, confident that he had remembered it correctly; sure that it would work magic, he opened his mouth and said:

'Plenty Marlboro king-size and Johnnie Walker Black Label plenty bottles.'

The translator looked at the army man, who smiled from behind his dark glasses. The soldiers looked at one another. Then the army man stepped up to Niakas and took him by the hand.

'Come with me,' he said to him in his own language. 'There are white men here who would like to hear what you have to say. Come!'

Niakas glanced at his companions. Now all were holding their hands over their privates. They stooped like old crones under the gaze of the soldiers.

Still, he thought. He had remembered the message of the man-who-speaks-to-the-canopy and the soldier had understood. Perhaps all would be well.

Niakas allowed himself to be led to the hut where the reporters had been taken. He repeated his message for them.

Walker and Van Drimmelen gazed blankly at Niakas as he repeated the sentence.

'There's your story,' said the army man.

On Fire for Guy

'What are you doing, Eric?' Benson asked, though he had a shrewd idea.

'November the fifth,' replied Eric in his squeaky voice which Benson found rather irritating.

Eric was pulling at a branch. It trailed behind him down the avenue, making a sad, autumnal, crackling sound.

Benson walked beside Eric, being careful not to let himself come into contact with the branch.

'I must tell you, Eric, that I and my family strongly disapprove of your celebrating Guy Fawkes Day the way you do. We consider it outrageous that you should burn a Catholic year after year.'

'It's good fun,' replied Eric, panting, his voice made even squeakier by his exertions.

'You Methodists have a peculiar idea of fun if you want my opinion,' Benson snapped back. 'We don't go about burning John Wesley even though he caused thousands – perhaps millions – to embrace the Protestant Heresy, and, therefore, no doubt, to lose their immortal souls.'

Eric stopped and let the branch fall. 'John Wesley never tried to blow up the Houses of Parliament,' he said.

'I bet he would've if they'd persecuted Methodists like they persecuted the poor Catholics.'

'My dad says,' said Eric, as he was often inclined to do, 'that Catholics have persecuted Protestants just as much.'

'I am sure your father tries hard to speak the truth, but THE TRUTH is embodied in the Catholic Church. If in the past

Catholics have occasionally been somewhat over-zealous in trying to persuade Pagans to see The Light then it was all in a good cause,' replied Benson dogmatically, as he was often inclined to be.

But Eric had lost interest. He lifted the branch again and trotted away without another word, disappearing down the side passage of his house, dragging the crackling branch behind him.

Benson went to his own garden and climbed the sycamore tree which afforded an excellent view of Eric's back garden. Looking down, he was shocked, appalled, to see a huge bonfire in the middle of the vegetable patch. Eric was busy heaving the branch on to the collection of wood, paper and garden clippings atop which sat Guy Fawkes. Guy was wearing a shirt, trousers and a trilby hat. His face had been painted on to a patched Frido football.

Benson shook his head sadly. It must be terrible, he thought, for Guy Fawkes to look down from heaven and see himself burnt all over England year after year. He heaved himself down from the tree and started to pray that it would rain like mad the following day, the fifth of November.

Benson, was a fat, fourteen-year-old boy, who felt that he was having a pretty thin time of it. In October he had failed to win a Certificate of Merit for religious knowledge, the first time in living memory that such a thing had occurred. The proud winner of this year's prize was Mahon, the son of a publican, whom, Benson reasoned, had used corrupt practices in order to obtain the prize. Brother O'Toole, Benson's form teacher – and a well-known wine-bibber – had been presented with a bottle of Irish Whiskey by Mahon the previous Christmas, while Benson had only brought Brother O'Toole a lavender bag to keep his hankies fresh.

So October had been a failure. Indeed nothing really good had happened to Benson since the summer fortnight in Rhyl and a spiritually uplifting excursion to St Winifred's Well in Holywell, where his wart had dropped off after a single dunk in the bubbling spring. The Methodists and other pagans in his avenue had November the fifth to carry them over to the next piece of spectacular sensation at Christmas. For them, Guy Fawkes Night was like a Milky Way between the two big meals of summer and Christmas. It didn't spoil your appetite but helped you get over the difficult flat, autumnal famine.

But Benson's dad said that fireworks were only for people with money to burn and anyway it was sinful to celebrate such a sad event as the death of a man. Mum, who was Italian, took up the theme happily. That was typical of the English, she said. The nearest they got to Carnival was standing around with their hands in their pockets in freezing temperatures to set off a few fireworks and frighten to death the poor pets they claimed to love so much the rest of the year.

So, for as long as Benson could remember, he had been forbidden to participate in the barbarous ritual. He had not even been allowed to observe the mischief from a distance. For some years he had protested his exclusion from the enjoyable time his friends were having, but for the last two years had swung towards militancy in things religious. He had been known to baptise his protestant friends in the Corporation baths – without their prior consent – reasoning that poor blind heathens should be forcibly brought into the fold for their souls' sake. He lectured them remorselessly on the theological niceties of the Trinity, transubstantiation and teleological proofs of the existence of God. If the Catholic Church was True – and Benson did not doubt for a moment that it was – then all the rest was lies and therefore Guy Fawkes Day ought not to be allowed. Q.E.D.

Before going to sleep that night, Benson once again prayed for rain, but Guy Fawkes Day dawned bright and clear and at school Benson scowled at the sun throughout the morning and afternoon as it travelled low from east to west across the southern sky in a most unseasonal fashion. As he dawdled home from school, the sun set and the stars came out one by one, crowding the sky for a better view of England's bonfires.

'It isn't right! Time is out of joint,' thought Benson as he walked down the avenue.

Out of the corner of his eye, he could see Eric's family having tea in the front room, but he did not look hard. Neither did he wave or nod as he passed. At the best of times social intercourse with protestants was a dubious pursuit, and today was far from being the best of times.

He opened the side door into the dark garden. The outdoor tap next to the garage wall banged his thigh – as it was often inclined to do – and Benson made a face and rubbed the spot, prior to giving the pipe from which the tap sprouted a good kick. 'That'll teach you, biffing me in the leg like that. As if I didn't have enough to put up with as it is.'

Then he suddenly had a flash of inspiration that made him tingle all over. He looked up at the expectant audience of the stars and knew that behind them, God, Jesus, Mary and all the saints had put the idea into his head. He even saw poor St Guy, sitting hunched on his cloud, perking up no end as news of the inspiration reached him.

Benson made his way across the garden, scaled the sycamore tree, and looked into Eric's garden. In the pitch dark, it took him a moment to make out the dark-grey wigwam shape of the bonfire with Guy Fawkes on top. He carefully aligned its position with the climbing rose on the fence between the two gardens. He got down from the tree and ran back into the garage. There he unrolled the hosepipe that dad had put away for the winter – thereby depriving his son of the use of the spool he loved to roll around the pavements of the County Borough. Benson felt about for the end of the hose with the nozzle attachment and screwed it tightly on to the tap. He took the other end to the fence and forced it between

two slats, estimating the correct angle of attack with all the 'O'
Level geometry at his command. The climbing rose pricked his
hand but Benson took no notice. Then, sending a final prayer
into the night, Benson ran back to the tap and turned it on full.

He could hear the water gushing and the rude sound of it
landing in Eric's graden. He worried whether it would be on
target, but then reasoned that if it were not on target Divine
Intervention would quickly make sure the virtuous mini-
climate, which Benson had been inspired to create to put an end
to wickedness, would miraculously divert the stream of water
over the bonfire to make sure it did a good job.

He stood panting next to the hissing tap in the dark. Then,
just as he had been scouting about for something else to do, the
light went on in the kitchen and he saw his mother making her
way to the sink. He started to worry then. Would there be time
for the abominable bonfire to get a good soaking before he was
called in for tea? Everything would have to be removed before
that, and before Eric's family came out for their satanic
celebrations.

But suddenly he was calm. Of course everything would work
out all right. The Lord had guided his hand. He was an
instrument of the Divine Will. He, Benson, fat, fourteen and
unworthy though he was, had been given the task of enforcing
righteousness.

So he took his time, stamped up and down against the cold
and imagined the sight of the miracle over the high fence.
Perhaps when Eric's family saw what had happened they
would see it as a sign and embrace the True Faith. No, that was
impossible. But then he looked up at the stars and his heart
started to pound faster until his ears were full of the sound.
If the stars were possible then anything was possible. He
imagined the headline in the Catholic Herald: SCHOOLBOY'S
INSPIRATION CONVERTS WHOLE AVENUE OF PAGANS!

He felt a poem coming on.

*

After tea, Benson sat righteously in the front room with all the lights on and the curtains open. Rockets cut across the sky and exploded into stars; Catherine wheels – once Benson's favourites because of their pious origins – whizzed around on electricity poles; rip-raps ripped around the children gathered in the cold avenue and rapped their din against his window. Benson did not look up. He sat, seemingly oblivious to the goings-on, busy polishing his poem, provisionally entitled *Death to Error*, while he awaited the spectacular damp squib of the grand finale.

It was nearly bedtime when the doorbell rang and Benson's dad answered it. Benson was drinking his Horlicks in the back room, while listening to his mum talking about her childhood in Bordighera, as she was often inclined to do.

He could hear Eric's dad talking to his dad. Then the door slammed shut and there was an ominous silence until dad came in and asked, 'Did you pour water on Eric's bonfire?'

'Yes, but I was an instrument of the Divine Will,' replied Benson piously.

'I'll give you instrument of the Divine Will,' said dad.

Martyred by abject apologies, but still unbowed, Benson lay in bed an hour later wondering about adults in general and his dad in particular. Didn't they realise that Truth had to be fought for? Why did they compromise all the time? Benson thought to himself, 'I'll never compromise! I am prepared to die for my beliefs just like Guy Fawkes. Tepid adults will get spat out, along with Methodists and other pagans. From now on I'll make Guy Fawkes my patron saint. After all, I've done my best for him, he's bound to want to return the favour.'

And Benson prayed: 'Oh, St Guy! You who were prepared to kill and die for your beliefs, help me to be on fire for Truth my whole life long! Do not let me become lukewarm like so many grown-ups.'

And Benson fell asleep right away, rocked by righteousness.

By the following evening the bonfire had dried out enough for Eric and his friends to set it alight. Benson's mum baked a rich Bordighera cake and donated it to Eric's mum as an ecumenical gesture.

'Live and let live, eh?' she said to Eric's mum.

Benson, out of sight, spent the jolly evening praying for rain and more than rain, for thunderbolts and lightning and unmistakable signs of the Godhead's displeasure. What was happening in the vegetable patch of Eric's garden was just plain *wrong*.

'Send just one little cloud to hover over the spot and dump tons of water on the pyre,' pleaded Benson. He also hoped that a voice from the cloud might boom out, 'I do this at the behest of that good boy, Benson, next door.'

But nothing of the sort happened. The stars stared down on stone-cold England, warmed a mite by Eric's bonfire, while Benson continued to seethe and boil and bubble and imagine the participants burning in a great everlasting bonfire as a punishment for their iniquities – as he listened to the carefree goings-on only a garden fence away.

Pitcher Plants

Dr Emmanuel Tabbi – President for Life, Wise Teacher, Subduer of the Great Grey Hippo of the Dicko River, Scourge of Colonial Running Sores and Post-Colonial Suppurating Pustules, Doctor of Creative Accountancy and Ditto of Indigenous Medicine – descended the rose granite staircase of his palace in Tabbitown. He walked resolutely and straight, noting with some satisfaction that his shoes were leaving deep footprints in the thick, apricot-coloured carpet which covered all the floors of the palace.

Dr Tabbi always insisted that his carpet be vacuumed against the lie of the pile in order that he could walk on it virgin each morning. To achieve this, the cleaners had to start on the ground floor and vacuum in retreat until they arrived at the last room on the top floor of the palace, from where they made an exit out of the window, proceeded along the roof parapet and down a fire-escape at the back of the building.

Never one to worry overmuch about the logistics involved in putting his whims into practice, Dr Tabbi gave not a thought to his cleaners' onerous routine. Rather, he was considering his forthcoming meeting with the Minister of Tourism for Porcellana, Edric Tabbi, B.A.

Peace had broken out in Porcellana after many years of fighting between the Oshunto tribe and the forces of the government. Porcellana, as is well known, has been formed on an island inhabited by two tribes: the Ung-Tabbi and the Oshunto. The Ung-Tabbi tribe, who occupy lands hugging the coastal plain, have always been the doers and movers, the masters of basic supply-side economics. The Oshunto tribe, on the other hand, live around the skirts of famed and fabled Mount Ruddock – named after a British Adventurer of the nineteenth century, Enid Ruddock, who had scaled it first in 1829. What the Oshunto did best was to engage in protracted worship of Mount Ruddock, perform various dark rituals to placate the spirits of ancestor, forest and mountain and, when not thus gainfully employed, raise goats with both the largest horns and the shortest legs in the world. Incidentally – though perhaps rather less than incidental for the lady concerned – Enid Ruddock disappeared mysteriously, having been forced to participate in one of the Oshunto's dark rituals during her descent of the peak. Enid's disappearance had – or so it was argued at the time – brought in the British, who were not, naturally, at all interested in the rubies and opals for which Porcellana was also even then justly famous. The unfortunate demise of Miss Ruddock, a matter of hours after the literal and metaphorical highpoint of an otherwise uneventful life, also explains, perhaps, why the British favoured the Ung-Tabbi during their colonial occupation, and gave them all the education and the first go at scholarships in England.

Upon gaining independence from Britain in 1963, war between the tribes had not taken long to flare up, and had been continuing ever since – until quite recently in fact – when Dr Emmanuel Tabbi had signed the Great Peace with the Oshunto. But what had puzzled Dr Tabbi, and many others concerned with the best interests of Porcellana, was how peace was to be preserved.

After much thought, Dr Tabbi felt he had come up with a solution. This he communicated to his Minister of Tourism, Edric Tabbi, that day.

'It is my intention, Minister-Cousin,' began Dr Tabbi, 'to exploit the potential of the Oshunto area for tourism. We shall provide the infrastructure and some basic skills training and let the Oshunto get on with it.'

The Minister of Tourism's eyes lit up. 'President-Cousin, I have just the company at hand who will complete the work.'

'The usual twenty per cent?' asked Dr Tabbi with a quiet smile, for he knew the talents of his cousin well.

'Naturally, President-Cousin. There was also talk of a free palace if we spent over twenty million jumpas.'

'Hmm. Please proceed. Get in touch with the Swedish Aid Bureau at once. I think they'll come up with the funds for such a worthwhile venture,' said Dr Emmanuel Tabbi.

Six months later a British couple arrived at a half-completed skyscraper hotel set in a clearing in the forest and wrapped around with mists swirling from Mount Ruddock.

Mr and Mrs Jefferson-Turner – Trevor and Harriet to their many friends in Esher – spent an uneasy night in the Isolde Tabbi suite. Harriet had been disturbed by the sound of Oshunto drumming and other noises from the mysterious dark. Trevor had spent most of the night in the bathroom trying to tune his Sony short-wave radio, bought at the Heathrow duty-free shop, to the BBC.

In the morning Harriet turned to Trevor and said, 'Did you hear the frogs last night?'

'Can't say I did,' replied Trevor. 'Couldn't even pick up the beeb.'

'Not those frogs, dear. The frogs outside the window.'

'Yes, now you come to mention it. I thought they might be cicadas or some such. Made the most frightful din.'

'Shame on you, Trevor!' chided Harriet, and she added, 'What time's the courtesy bus coming?'

Trevor snorted.

'What does that mean, Trevor?'

'Well, a bus may come, my dear, but courtesy I do not expect in Porcellana. Remember how they manhandled us into the so-called courtesy airport pick-up?'

Harriet told Trevor that he was a bad traveller and continued to apply her sun-screen. She applied it liberally, ending in a final smear of Australian Beach Paint in a violent violet shade.

'Going native, Harriet?' Trevor asked her.

Trevor and Harriet Jefferson-Turner had decided, along with a group of fifteen Japanese, to test the waters of Porcellanan tourism by climbing Mount Ruddock. What had motivated Trevor and Harriet to do this was a feeling that there were no places left to visit. Thailand, once their great love, had become overrun; they knew every lion and elephant in the Serengeti by name; and if they saw another sunset over Ayers Rock, they felt certain that they would expire of ennui. So the discrete advertisement in the *Telegraph* had come at exactly the right time – just when they had thought there was not only no place like home but no place but home. Apart from the promise of being able to scale the fourth highest mountain in the southern hemisphere, they were also anxious to view the pitcher plants that were said to grow in profusion on the mountainside.

What had brought the fifteen Japanese was, as ever, closed to enquiry.

The guides from the Oshunto tribe, dressed in neatly pressed khaki shorts, had inwardly licked their lips when they beheld the tourists and the heavy suitcases on castors being rolled across the rough concrete floor of the Oshunto Dawn Hotel. While the hotel was being built, these guides had been sat down under the trees and treated to a crash course in hotel and tourist English. At first they had not taken to the idea of shunting 'obootees' – a term which might be translated as 'foreigners', but which also denotes 'those pale imitations of the Oshunto who have never trod the mountain' – through their homeland. However, the sight of the bemused foreigners arriving with their suitcases full of useful items had enthused them for the enterprise.

The following day at dawn, after a day and a night of climbing,

Trevor and Harriet and the fifteen Japanese stood on the summit of Mount Ruddock, surrounded by five Oshunto guides.

The sun rose predictably through the ocean of cloud far below them and the Japanese clicked away with a variety of sophisticated cameras while Harriet and Trevor sat motionless contemplating the scene; thinking how wonderful it was; how irritating the clicking, buzzing, whirring cameras of the Japanese were; wondering if this shared experience would breathe new life into their marriage.

Trevor said, 'In a few years this place will be overrun.'

Harriet nodded. 'I can't help thinking of Uncle Arthur,' she said.

'I know what you mean.'

Harriet's Uncle Arthur had been in a Japanese prisoner-of-war camp and now lived on the Wirral peninsula in a house that contained not one single Japanese product.

Trevor stood up and stretched.

'Careful, dear!' counselled Harriet. 'It's a shocking drop.'

'Certainly is,' agreed Trevor, contemplating the sheer falling away of the granite from the summit. 'Wonder how deep the gully is.'

'The brochure says it drops for a thousand metres or so.'

'Does it indeed?' observed Trevor, eyeing the gully accusingly for having the impertinence to drop so far while he was in the vicinity.

'The pitcher plants were wonderful, weren't they?' Harriet said.

'Absolutely. But one has to feel just a little bit sorry for the poor insects, ending up being gobbled down by a plant. It doesn't seem right somehow. An insect is a step up from a plant in my book. Shouldn't be allowed to be eaten by a lower form of life.'

'Yes, but we get eaten by worms,' observed Harriet.

'Not until we're dead.'

'It's all a matter of nature being red in tooth and claw. They ventured where they shouldn't. Not evolved enough to leave well alone. Until they do, the pitcher plants will make a meal of them,' Harriet stated, with some relish.

'You're a hard woman, Harriet.'

'You wouldn't have me any other way,' purred back Harriet, taking Trevor's hand and burying her long nails into his soft palm.

Harriet and Trevor were silent after that as they contemplated the continuing dawn light-show taking place in front of them. So rapt were they that they did not at first notice the increased volume of the Japanese voices behind them. When they did, they whispered to one another such well-used phrases as 'Typical!' 'What can you expect!' 'Dead from the neck up!' 'No souls!' But they did not deign to turn round and so did not see that the Oshunto guides had corralled the Japanese with a long piece of sisal rope, and were pulling them together across the flat summit of Mount Ruddock, towards the place where Harriet and Trevor sat on the edge of the gully. Only when the first Japanese fell down the precipice to their immediate right were they aware that the Oshunto guides, their eyes hard and glittering, their heads full of expensive luggage-on-castors back in the hotel rooms at the base of their mountain, were sacrificing the tourists to their old gods.

Harriet and Trevor looked at one another as Japanese tourists and their cameras lost their footing all around them and fell with the screams of kamikaze pilots into the ether.

Then the rope tightened around Trevor and Harriet.

'I say! Now look here!' reproved Trevor, as if he were addressing a recalcitrant trade unionist. But Harriet did not say anything. She could only think of the insects plopping into the open mouths of the pitcher plants. The rope was digging into her, pushing her inexorably towards the chasm.

An Oshunto guide kept repeating, 'You're welcome, madam! With pleasure, madam! That'll do nicely, madam! Have a good day, madam!' as he came closer and closer, wearing a really quite pleasant smile, a smile belied by the corset rope and the threatening angle at which he held his machete.

Soon the summit of Mount Ruddock had returned to its customary calm. The Oshunto guides made their way back down the mountain, their thoughts anchored on windfall profits.

A few months later, Dr Emmanuel Tabbi sat in the rumpus room of his new palace. He smiled at the view of fabled Mount Ruddock through the window. War had recommenced between the Ung-Tabbi and the Oshunto and was being conducted with rather more vigour than previously. The world – well, the Japanese government and the Esher Conservative Association – had protested vociferously about the untoward treatment meted out to their trailblazing tourists. Offers of aid had been numerous, the only provision of which had been that the money should be devoted to punitive war on the now-hated Oshunto tribe. President Tabbi obliged with alacrity. It was all very satisfactory. The Oshunto Dawn Hotel provided excellent billeting for his troops. The spare twenty per cent he put aside for his forthcoming European tour.

But as Dr Emmanuel Tabbi surveys Mount Ruddock through tinted double-glazed patio doors, an Oshunto warrior, harried by troops and retreating ever farther up the slopes of the mountain – wearing the identity brooch of a Japanese tourist in his hair, Harriet's Hermes headscarf around his loins – looks up towards the summit where thunder crashes and lightning flashes, placating the old gods – and some new ones – with chants. The jungle swallows him up, the tribesman and his nearly new Samsonite flight bag.

The sun sets and President Tabbi toasts its departure with a glass of Mr Suzuki's Scotch. He tunes in Trevor's Sony to 'Porcellan Pops with Pam'. He sighs with satisfaction, then searches in Mr Yamaguchi's lightweight linen jacket for a pack of Mr Mitsuda's Mild Seven cigarettes. He lights one with Harriet's Mappin and Webb lighter and watches the smoke as it snakes away towards Mount Ruddock on the Poison – courtesy of Mrs Minagawa – scented air.

The Buddha's Mattress

The sun slinks away. A single crane ascends from the reed-bed below my garden. It flies low over the bay. For a split second I can see two cranes. One in the sky. One in the water. Then both have disappeared into the rays of the sun. I raise my glass to my lips again. I search for the crane. Touches of red tint sky and sea. The day dies smiling.

In the garden Seung-Il and Jung-Ja, who are my father and mother, brother and sister, son and daughter, pause from their work to watch the sea. Seung-Il's mattock leans against his thigh. Jung-Ja removes her hat to wipe her brow. They are still. They do not speak. A moment ago, when the crane left, they were bent double, preparing the vegetable garden. Now as I watch they return to their work. Soon it will be time for me to prepare tea for them.

I am drunk again. But I am drunk as a skylark is drunk. When Seung-Il and Jung-Ja come into the kitchen for tea they will remark on how unsteadily I hold the pot. I will smile and shrug. Perhaps Jung-Ja will touch my hand. Certainly Seung-Il will smile . . .

The kitchen cupboard is bare. My family's needs are few. A tea-caddy stands alone in the cupboard above the stove. The teapot and tiny cups are arranged on the scrubbed table, a father surrounded by his children. I fill the kettle and listen to the sound of water falling into it. I see the light of day dying in the kitchen. The room smells of drying clothes. There is also an aroma of hot newspaper.

It is lucky I noticed the pile of newspapers. I bend with

difficulty to move them away from the heat. The smell pricks me into a reluctant memory of Len. Len used to leave his paper near the fire to protect his knees from the blast. Len, my second stab at building a bridge over Loneliness River. I liked Len because he made me feel calm. I was not calm, you understand. But Len was as jumpy as a hummingbird and made me seem a seer, a guru, in comparison.

The kettle whistles. I let it go on, thinking of Seung-Il and Jung-Ja. Through the window I can see them making their way up the garden path; behind them banks of crimson cloud. I feel unutterably happy. I suppose it is partly the wine I have been drinking. But only partly. The real reason for my happiness is coming up the garden path. I must set about preparing their tea.

Seung-Il and Jung-Ja and their two children, Seung-Chun and Heng-Hoon, are watching television now. They watch anything and everything. Still, it is an innocent vice. Without it perhaps they would become homesick. That must be prevented at all costs.

It is dark now. Curls of cloud cover the sky and veil the stars. I fill the Aga before setting about cooking our evening meal. We are having curry tonight. It's Monday.

It was a Monday when I arrived in Seoul all those years ago. I was drunk then too. The taxi driver must have scented it.

'You want girl?' he asked.

'No, thank you,' I replied, amused at the very idea and how, wherever I went, I was asked that question by a turning head in the dark.

'Boy?' he asked.

'Er . . . no. Thank you. I want the Je-Ju Hotel.'

But he took me around and around.

It took me a while to realise that I was participating in the universal taxi driver ritual by which strangers the whole world over are made to feel more strange. Seoul through the window fascinated me but then I realised that I recognised a street because a neon sign for 'Dunhill' had lost its 'H' and had thereby been Koreanised 'Dun-Ill'. The first time I passed it I was amused. The second time perplexed. The third time angry. But I let it happen. I decided to see how far the man would dare to go. I resolved that on no account would I mention the fact that the journey was taking too long. I was on my holiday after all. I had money in my pocket. Why, I had enough money in my pocket to see me out. Twenty years in the desert, though it had put my soul to death, had also enriched me beyond the wildest dreams of accountants. I, barely fifty, could retire! And I could allow myself a small expenditure to test the corruption of a taxi-driver to its hilt.

The sight of the city was, in the main, not a pretty one. The war, though long over, still scarred the place and this dereliction had been exacerbated by the frenzied rush to develop. Coming as I was from Singapore, which had had longer to put on paint and a smiling face, I was startled by the state of Seoul. Its whole population appeared to be on the street, watching my taxi pass.

After the third circuit, I concentrated on the back of the taxi driver's head. I was peculiarly moved by it. I told myself that this was due to jet-lag, but the man's thick, black hair, cut abruptly short to expose a naked neck so thin that one could not believe it could carry his head, produced a pity in me. He seemed as vulnerable as a jar of honey left open in a jungle.

We continued for maybe forty-five minutes. Then the driver asked me, 'What you want?'

I shrugged and smiled at him.

It was a fair question. What did I want? Had he asked me that thirty years before I might have answered, 'I want someone to love, and a well-paying job and a sense of accomplishment.' But now I could only smile and hope that the smile was Buddha-like and serene, though I felt the corners of my mouth downward-pulling and my chin quivering like a child's.

He turned off the main roads. These had been dimly lit at best, but the ones he now drove along were almost pitch-black. Our headlights showed obscenely overblown against the pin pricks of candles-in-saucers – lights emanating from the hovels we were passing. He did not speak again.

At last we stopped in front of a nondescript clapperboard hovel. He put the handbrake on with a gesture of great finality. I became frightened suddenly, no longer suave and in charge, and almost broke my promise to myself. The question, 'Is this the Je-Ju hotel?' bubbled up in my throat but I did not speak.

The driver got out of the car and disappeared into the hovel. He was gone a long time. I sat, wondering what was planned for me, thinking that this might easily be my death for all I knew. It would be so easy for them to take me, rob me and leave me somewhere. Would anybody worry about the corpse of a fat foreigner amidst the chaos of Seoul?

But at last he returned and gestured for me to follow him into the hovel. I did this without any complaint. I remember that I wondered why I was so pliable, why I had made this resolution to follow passively through to the end. In fact I still wonder. And when I wonder, I bless my mood – or whatever it was – that made me stubborn and determined to follow this inscrutable man to the limits of his will.

I followed him into a room, perhaps the only room in the hovel. It smelled of Kimchy, the Korean obsession, a kind of pickled cabbage, but I could not put a name to the smell then. It also smelled of poverty, a pungent smell of babies and damp and sweat and milky sweetness, a smell that is totally international.

The room, lit by a single white candle, contained a mattress on the floor and a small stool. The driver told me to enter the room and sit on the stool. I took my shoes off. He saw what I had done and smiled. Then he disappeared.

I sat down. The night air was full of insects which kept colliding with the candle. I began to warn them, I remember,

'Don't!' but my voice buzzed darkly in the air and after that I centred my gaze on the mattress, wondering what part it would play in the proceedings, and fearing the worst. I told myself I could make an excuse and leave, lighter by a few dollars, but in one piece.

Then it occurred to me that making an excuse and leaving had been my whole life. Gwen had been left even though she had protested her love and said that sex wasn't the most important thing. I sent her dollars while she involved herself in good works in Salisbury. Then, when I thought I knew where I stood and took up with Len, Len had been left too. 'I'm only popping round the corner to Arabia for a mo. I won't be long! We need the money!' But I had never gone back and Len, who had said that I was the best thing that had ever happened to him, had spoken true by jumping under a train and ending the confusion that had so strangled his poor brain and had made me feel calm in comparison.

I sat on.

I do not know how much time passed. The grey mattress had become a screen on which I saw my life being replayed at speed. As I watched each scene of it unfold, I remember being acutely conscious that I was witnessing something which, people assured me, was generally only seen by those about to die. I neither believed nor disbelieved this. There was an urge to find out. I saw my villa in Portugal. It was there, now, ready, waiting for me to see the world and pronounce it 'done'; the garden stretching down to the sea anxious for the love and care the dotty bachelor with the monthly interest cheques from England would be prepared to extend it. But as soon as the image of each room had meandered across the dirty mattress, it too was gone into memory, as insubstantial as the endless hours of sums I had suffered through in Arabia in order to acquire it.

Then the film seemed to blur. I saw myself running, running over dunes. They could have been the dunes of Normandy or the dunes of the Rub Al Khali. I did not know. I only knew that I was running. And then the mattress grew blank and I saw its stains in the candlelight and mused that mattress stains the world over tell a similar story of loneliness and single tickets.

I do not know how much time had passed, when, silently, into the room they came. They stood in front of me, this girl and boy, no more than seventeen years of age, smiling. There was no sign of the driver.

I smiled back but that only killed their smiles. They turned to one another and slowly began removing their ragged clothes. The girl was diminutive and not particularly attractive. She wore a cotton dress, thin and faded with overwashing. It slipped over her head with the help of the boy. The boy was tall and thin, a thinness that made me doubt how such a small space could contain all the organs and gristle of life. His ribs showed through his torso.

At last they stood in front of me pathetically naked, smiling grotesquely. I did not say anything. I think I was more amused than anything else by the absurdity of the situation. I knew that I did not want to see what I knew would follow. Nearby a dog barked and then growled. Another dog whimpered, then screamed in pain and suddenly a chorus of barks and growls, as made by a whole pack of dogs, filled the room. I watched what followed on the mattress from my stool, detached, like some fat Buddha.

But nothing much happened. Starved of protein, shriveled further by my presence, the couple simulated lust impotently. Then, quite suddenly, the girl began to cry. She turned her face away from the boy and whimpered into the mattress. He stared down at her for a long moment and then I saw tears falling from his cheekbones in heavy drops upon the girl's breast. His arms collapsed and he lay upon her body and wept too.

In their weeping they were oblivious of me. I looked at them for perhaps a minute, thinking it was part of the show; that they knew me and knew that I would be moved to pity and dive deeper into my fat pocket as a result. But the tears of the couple increased. They were, I knew, totally self-contained in their union of sorrow.

I had ceased to exist.

I could only surmise as to what was the cause of their grief. Poverty, war memories, the daily hunt for food, shame at the work they had managed to find. The tears they were shedding were wasting hard-earned calories. The mattress was soaking it up as it had soaked up so much before.

And I cried too. At first I whimpered for the memories of my life, so recently enacted on the screen of the mattress, now brought to life writhing upon it, frustrated and hopeless. I wept for myself and for the life wasted in running away in order to give myself a safe old age in a too-big house. I whimpered and then I bawled like a girl or like a baby or like a muezzin in a minaret or like the dog outside.

My weeping startled the couple on the bed. They looked towards me. They stood up and came to either side of me with a questioning expression on their tear-stained faces. The girl held out her hand and touched me on the shoulder. The boy stroked away tears from my cheek. His thin hand made a grating sound as it stroked my beard.

I smiled and dried my eyes.

'Can you help me to find the Je-Ju Hotel?' I asked them.

The sun has long since set. The sky is alive with stars. Jung-Ja is putting the children to bed. Seung-Il is writing to his family in Seoul. He wants us to visit them. We shall but I fear they may not want to return after a visit. I fear that as most people fear death.

Soon we shall go for a swim off the jetty at the end of the garden, my family and I. The phosphorescence will fall off our bodies like jewels. Jung-Ja says that the gleaming phosphorescences in the water are dead stars. And it is true that the pin-pricks of light are just like the moving lights above our heads. Jung-Ja has many strange ideas, however. She says that clouds are the Buddha's mattress. I do not contradict or tell her that they are water vapour, for then she would simply say that they are the ocean's tears.